THE FAMISHED GODS

Speaking Selves in *Akkarmashi*

Dr. Praveen Kumar Anshuman
Ravi Prakash Chaubey

Pharos Books

ISBN: 978-93-89843-70-5
eISBN: 978-93-89843-71-2

©Publishers

Publisher: Pharos Books (P) Ltd.
Plot No.-55, Main Mother Dairy Road
Pandav Nagar, East Delhi-110092
Phone: 011-40395855
WhatsApp: +91 8447931000
E-mail: sales@pharosbooks.in
Website: www.pharosbooks.in
Edition: 2020 (Second)
Cover Design: Virendra Singh Bhandari
Inner Design: Surendra Kumar

The Famished Gods
Author: Dr. Praveen Kumar Anshuman
(Email ID: pkanshuman@kmc.du.ac.in; M.: +91 9999851780)
Ravi Prakash Chaubey
(Email ID: ravipchaube@gmail.com; M.: +91 8802161429)

"The originality of their book, " The Famished Gods", is that its authors, Praveen Kumar Anshuman and Ravi Prakash Chaubey, have used a very innovative methodology of analyzing and understanding dalit experience and life, basing their study on "Akkarmashi", the subaltern ethno autobiography of the distinguished Marathi dalit writer, Sharankumar Limbale. Underlying in this seminal book is the working of the brahminic ideology which sees to it that dalits, the Gods who create food and wealth with their blood and sweat, are kept famished with their stomachs eternally aching with hunger, that they, the labourers, are kept divided and disunited into sub castes by injecting the poisonous notions of purity and pollution in their food habits, that the upper-caste males can prey up on hungry dalit women to satisfy their lust with impunity. The authors unravel and unmask these and many such strategies used by the upper castes to exploit and oppress dalits. This book is a must read for anyone who cares for the liberation and empowerment of dalits."

- Bama, a Renowned Dalit Novelist and author of her famous autobiography, 'Karukku'

About the Editors

Dr. Praveen Kumar Anshuman is working as Assistant Professor in the Department of English at Kirori Mal College, University of Delhi for the last ten years. He did his Ph.D. from Banaras Hindu University. He has published five books- *Stoppardian Coconuts: Soft Within though Hard Without, Changing Complexion of Delhi: A Study of Jhuggi-Jhopdi Cluster and Cultural Transition, Ecosensibilities: Finding Path to Harmony, Aakhar Sovat Naahin,* and *Maanush Jaagat Naahin. The Famished Gods: Speaking Selves in Akkarmashi* is his sixth book that deals with Sharankumar Limbale's autobiography, *Akkarmashi: The Outcaste,* through a critical lens.

Ravi Prakash Chaubey is a Research Fellow at the School of Language, Literature and Culture Studies, Jawaharlal Nehru University, New Delhi. He did his M.Phil. from the same University. He completed his graduation from St. Stephen's College, University of Delhi. He has published two books- *Aakhar Sovat Naahin* and *Maanush Jaagat Naahin.* The present volume is his third book.

Disclaimer

This is to acknowledgement that Dr. Praveen Kumar Anshuman and Ravi Prakash Chaubey (a Faculty member at the Department of English, Kirori Mal College, University of Delhi and a Research Fellow at the School of Language, Literature, and Culture Studies, Jawaharlal Nehru University, respectively) are the joint editors of this book 'The Famished Gods: Speaking Selves in *Akkarmashi*'. The editors have done their best in doing the plagiarism check and the other related things while publishing this volume. To the best of their knowledge, the chapters included in this book by the contributors are original but if, in any case, they are found having done the plagiarism or published elsewhere or the like, the sole responsibility shall fall on the contributors. The editors shall bear no responsibility with regard to the same along with the views expressed by them in their chapters. The editors' major efforts have been in compiling and bringing a good material on *Akkarmashi: The Outcaste* for the students as well as the researchers.

Dedicated to my Baba (Grandfather),
Swargeeya Shri Hargun Ram,
the greatest inspiration of my village, Poorab Patti, Durbasa, Azamgarh

- Dr. Praveen Kumar Anshuman

Dedicated to my Baba ji
Swargeeya Shri Shiv Kumar Chaubey

- Ravi Prakash Chaubey

Preface to the Second Edition

Writing Preface to the second edition of our book, 'The Famished Gods: Speaking Selves in *Akkarmashi*' and that too within a month from its first publication has given us joy which is in fact indescribable in spirit. We are deeply indebted to the love and affection, expressed by our readers across the whole country. Mr. Sharankumar Limbale, the author of the autobiography, *The Outcaste*, on which ours has been the very first critical assessment, has himself expressed his happiness on the success stories that this edition is narrating every moment.

It is our great pleasure that DU teachers have taken good efforts in recommending the book to the college libraries. Besides, the students who are not studying this paper in their honours courses have also taken keen interest in reading it with great appreciation. Among many others, Dr. Durgesh Upadhyaya from Kashi Vidyapith, Dr. Kumar Vimlendu Singh, a distinguished poet and scholar and Ms. Saumya Darshana, an avid reader, are the ones who, despite having different areas of interest, loved our book very much. Dr. Satya Prakash Prasad's invitation for the book discussion at Jamia Millia Islamia was another value addition imparted to our work.

We as the editors have really toiled hard in this academic endeavour of ours, which in its first edition resulted as *The Famished Gods* has been loved by thousands of readers and scholars. Similarly, the upcoming two volumes, *Casting out the Caste: Akkarmashi, the Outcaste* and *Depressed Deities: Aching Selves in Akkarmashi*, we hope, will also be able to take the interests of the readers on the go, and serve them in exploring Limbale's autobiography with more profoundness and clarity.

Contents

Acknowledgement

It is a matter of great pleasure that the efforts of brining a book of a concretely cognizant altitude in Dalit Studies has finally fructified in *The Famished Gods: Speaking Selves in Akkarmashi*. As life is a combinatorial gamut of interconnectedness, synchronicity, and concord, so is the case with all forms and fabrics present within and without.

This book came to be conceptualized after meeting with the renowned writer in the realm of Dalit Litearure, Shri **Sharankumar Limbale** at Sahitya Academy, New Delhi. Interacting with him there on various issues related to literature, life, and academics brought our focus on his famous autobiography *Akkarmashi: The Outcaste*, which has dearth of any crtitical book in English though it has exuberantly invited many works of criticism in Marathi language. This resulted into an assignment given to us by the grace of the author of the book himself for which we the editors shall always be indeted. We thank Limbale sir from the bottom of our heart, for in the process of editing this volume we went through many stages of knowing the covert dimentions of our society which are very much real and tangibly alive in our present society.

At the very outset, I, Praveen Kumar Anshuman, would love to remember my English teachers **Shri D.C. Srivastatava** (DAVIC, Azamgarh), **Prof. J.S. Jha** (BHU), **Prof. S.N. Pandey** and **Prof. R.N. Rai** (Both retired from BHU) whose blessings keep always showering on me unconditionally. I express my deep gratitude towards the great luminary in the field of Political Science, **Prof. Shriprakash Singh** (DU), whose unconditional support at all levels keep me going ahead with great zeal and enthusiasm.

Alongwith Dr. Anshuman, I, Ravi Prakash Chaubey, would also like to express my deep regards for a few personalities without the blessings of whom I could not have travelled even an inch. They are – **Swargeeya Shiv Kumar Chaubey** (Baba), **Swargeeya Sarayu Prasad Gupta** (my English teacher), **Smt. Premshila Devi** (my mother) and **Prof. Deo Shankar Navin** (my Ph.D. Supervisor). It would be an act of great remorsefulness if I do not mention the name of my Big B, **Dr. Praveen Kumar Anshuman**, whom I have an indescribable bond with.

We, both the Editors, would like to express deep sense of gratitude to all the contributors— **Ms. Deepna Rao, Ms. Surina Mol R., Ms. Sonali Rode, Mr. Darshan Lal, Ms. Bidisha Pal, Ms. Charu Arya, Ms. Yasmeena Jan, Mr. Binu K.D., and Ms. Anne Placid** —who have taken the deep concern very sincerely to the utmost possibility and endeavored in the right spirit in bringing out their latent research acumen in a tangibly concrete form as manifested in this book.

Finally, a very special word of thanks to **Mr. Shashikant 'Sadaiv'** with all his team members like **Mr. Surendra Kumar (Graphic Designer)** and others for their painstaking interest in our work and publishing it with his firm, Pharos Books Pvt. Ltd.

We hope the book would be able to do justice to the cause for which the efforts have been accelerated in genuine setting.

Foreword

The muffled voices of the *Dalit* and marginalised have often been appropriated by the grandiloquent bigwigs of the elitist discourse with impunity since time immemorial. Efforts have been made to mythicize the caste realities and the oppressions faced by *the outcaste*s in simplified binaries to elicit sympathetic responses from the readers by a generation of mainstream writers. They conveniently discount the multiplicity of complex psycho-social and socio-economic dynamics which are, in fact, at the core of *Dalit* identity and its discourse. Sharankumar Limbale's *Akkarmashi: The Outcaste*, therefore, assumes greater significance as an auto-narrative encapsulating the harsher realties of social stratagems which a *Dalit* is compelled to forbear every nanosecond of his/her life immaterial of upward social and economic mobility of the individual.

I express my happiness and satisfaction at Dr. Anshuman's efforts with Mr. Ravi Prakash Chaubey in bringing out the present book, *The Famished Gods: Speaking Selves in Akkarmashi*. The title of the book itself makes it amply clear that the issues explored in its pages has an empathetic overtones and it has an objective to cater to its readers a worldview that is largely relegated to the background. I see it as an endeavour to foreground and expose the visible and invisible fetters as well as ensnares that dehumanise subjects getting stigmatized and trapped owing to their caste identity.

The contributors have been upright in probing the issues from multiple perspectives like the intricacies of caste system, harrowing lived experience faced by an illegitimate child, orthodoxies of Indian society, fossilization of caste system, domination of socio-political affair of the contemporary world, theorization of aesthetics of Dalit Literature, different metaphors of food, memories and histories of the marginalized, the identity and existential crisis, in-betweenness of the central character, the cusp of liminality and sub-liminality, autobiographical articulation of Dalit consciousness, Dalit resistance through body, dissent against caste, multiple addressability, non-linear narration, internal probing and self-criticism and many more.

In the light of above, I don't have any hesitation to aver that the book, *The Famished Gods: Speaking Selves in Akkarmashi* is a faithful exhibit of literary and critical endeavor to cater the perceptive and enthusiastic minds of the readers and whet their research acumen objectively. The book certainly draws the eclecticism and multiple approaches to decode the embedded realities which are largely overlooked through the overarching and seemingly innocuous simplifications. The critical insights presented by the contributors shall undoubtedly stir the research orientation of prospective students of literature in the areas of Dalit literature and the Writings from the Margin. I congratulate the editors of the book, especially my loving brother, Dr. Praveen Kumar Anshuman, for his endeavor and wish him all success in his upcoming academic and research engagements and personal life.

- **Dr. Satya Prakash Prasad**
Faculty at the Department of Humanities & Social Sciences
Jamia Millia Islamia, New Delhi

Introduction

Akkarmashi or The Outcaste (2003), originally written in Marathi by Sharankumar Limbale and translated by Santosh Bhoomkar is an autobiographical account of the renowned writer in Dalit Studies, Sharankumar Limable. This book gives the details of excruciating experiences of the narrator who suffers double out-caste-ness for being an offspring of sexual exploitation of a lower caste woman by a high caste Patil. It digresses from the set conventions of autobiographical writings in that the self and the community is analogously narratavized. As a subaltern ethno-biography, *The Outcaste* is characterised by genuineness of experience and expression, articulation of Dalit consciousness, centrality of Dalit body, dissent against caste, multiple addressability, non-linear narration, internal probing and self-criticism. Limbale, through the medium of autobiography, has effected a re-inscription of Dalit cultural identity, using the locus of the Dalit insider.

The present volume of *The Famished Gods: Speaking Selves in Akkarmashi* is a microscopic scrutiny from the dimension crucial to generally marginalized sections of Indian society and that is the perpetual situation of penury and destitution at the heart of which remains nevertheless indubiously the stomach working as the metaphor since time immemorial. Sharankumar Limbale's seminal work, his famous autobiography, *Akkarmashi: The Outcaste*, has multifarious aspects which require proper attention. The present book focuses the said metaphor of stomach that stands for a life hovering around food narrating the story of hunger. Food and Hunger, it is evident, remain like a throbbing impulse in the entire body of the text. This work accentuates mainly on hunger and secondarily drives attention on the other related dimensions which do not move out farther away from the destined approaches. Apart from the well researched chapters from scholars of deep understanding of the text, the book also includes an adequate list of glossary that describes particularly the regional vocabulary in lucid fashion to grasp an easy understanding for its readers.

The first chapter - *Exploring the Leitmotifs of Food* - explores the grim reality of poverty in the Mahar community. This chapter majorly deals with the theme of Dalit poverty where familial solidarity is highlighted through the leitmotifs of food and hunger. This chapter seeks to explore these leitmotifs, while highlighting the aesthetics of Dalit Literature as outlined the author himself. Additionally, it presents the fresh critical perspective of Gastro-criticism of Dalit Writing. This chapter further provides readers with a new vista for a deeper understanding of Dalit aesthetics, namely the leitmotifs of food and hunger. Additionally, it engenders a mode of looking at technical elements of Dalit writing and an appreciation of Dalit literary craft and style, as the technique of writing is closely interwoven with important thematic discussions. Thirdly, it enables an understanding of how hunger is an important element of deprivation in Dalit existence, and a condition that contributes largely towards the poor quality of life. Fourthly, it provides fresh insights into the characters of the novel, and decision-making that is driven by the exigencies of hunger and basic subsistence. It is seen that the element of hunger allows one to reassess the characters' moral choices and questionable acts, and view both the criminal and illegal activities of the novel in a new light, where ethics clash with survival instincts. Finally, the societal neglect of the Dalits may also be evaluated through the leitmotifs of food and hunger.

The second chapter - *Inscription of Casteism through Stomach* - enumerates a real life narrative which addresses the malignant system of casteism in Indian society in a bildungsroman fashion. The different memories of Sharan that traverses through his family, village and wider social platforms, driven by Dalit activism expose the structural foundations of casteism like occupation, religion and food. This chapter traces out the different metaphors of food which make it possible to narrate the memories and histories of the marginalized community. It is connected to the domestic and public realms; consequently the personal memories of food get a political dimension here. The food practices in his community are a confused category that etches the difficulty of existence of a Dalit whose lineage is fraught with chaos. Hunger is the reality and the food choices of the community arose because of the necessity of survival in a society where the economical and social privileges favour the (so-called) upper caste. Consequently, meat eating and non-vegetarian diet were seen as pollution, the fear of which is crept into the various sub castes inside the untouchables thus finalizing the varna system in Hindu society. The binary of purity/impurity deconstructs food as a material category and makes us aware of its scarcity, deprivation, the tradition of storing and preserving food as well as the ways of finding and serving food etc. In this chapter, food also becomes a site where gender intersections are also played. The perception of food by women, men and upper castes are also given thrust. Food is also a site of resistance and revolution where the explicit and implicit inscription of casteism is foregrounded.

The third chapter - *Hunger and Exploitation* – expresses the bitterness and deprivation in the life of the characters of the text, recording the cruelty of India's caste system. It espouses change and transformation of the society in order to overcome the wrong beliefs and inequalities which fling humanity into perilous state affairs. Further, this chapter observes the social and political worlds through insightful senses of the author. Even after the independence the caste ridden India fails to terminate caste difference. This chapter makes an effort to have clear contemporary relevance, even considering the current dynamism of Indian social relationship.

The fourth chapter - *A Tale of Ceaseless Atrocities* - deals with the 'self-lived' experiences of different characters in a realistic manner. It documents the intricacies of caste system and the most harrowing lived experiences faced by an illegitimate child. It also registers the experiences of an untouchable family in general and Dalit community in particular against poverty, hunger and exploitation. It highlights how Dalit women who are the most sufferers in the text are exploited inside the house by their own men and outside by upper caste people. They submit meekly to their exploiters like dumb cattle. Besides this, the chapter is a document of the struggle of an outcaste against the rotten patriarchal society and his struggle for identity and social equality. This chapter also registers Dalits' incessant struggle for identity and against hunger and poverty.

The fifth chapter - *The Contested Identities* - expounds the concept of identity and existential crisis. As Dalit autobiographies, being more of communal biographies than individual autobiographies construct the formation of the social identity of an individual, *The Outcaste* is an embodiment of fractured identity of an individual who is as an akkarmashi or half-caste because of being born of lower caste Mahar mother and an upper caste Patil father. Apart from presenting the very dalitized identity and existential crisis of his community people and his family, the narrative journey produces contested moments of afflictions and uneasiness of the narrator who belongs to neither the lower caste nor the upper caste but on the juncture of liminality and sub-liminality. The process of identity transformation causes further dilemma.

The sixth chapter - *Voices of the Self* - is an intense account of describing trauma of a fatherless, casteless writer. The caste narration as depicted by the text reveals trauma of being born into a Dalit community in 'modern times?' through the decision of penning down his voice. Caste compresses and brings him into the state of constant suffering and forces him to be a non reacting phenomenon towards his identity. Being an outcaste and a dalit, Sharan goes through a traumatic childhood, full of hunger and regular stigmatic encounters in the identity-less community. His loss of faith in motherhood and regular striving for the name of father becomes the reason for his increased trauma. He finds himself helpless when his surname is scrutinized behind attacks on sexuality and immorality of his mother. His pain and trauma of being fatherless while he questions the inhuman treatment he received from the upper caste people leads to increases his suffering further. The chapter further represents many other characters, which are born as a result of such illicit carnal relations between upper caste men and lower caste women. He is voicing the helplessness and surrender of many other women of his community. How sex becomes the source of survival for all such women and how this has been psychologically commented upon by the protagonist has been debated in this chapter. His education later shows him path to connect with divine figures and historical heroes. He identifies himself with their power as he has been powerless throughout his life. And this quest leaves him into regular questioning with regard to his identity while finding relief in a different religion, Buddhism.

The seventh chapter - *Layers of Resistance* - portrays the pain, suffering and humiliation of Dalits in India. It narrates the story of a child born to Dalit mother, who was raped by the upper caste man. The offspring out of this conjugation bearing the fractured identity suffered its entire life for having no identity of its own, no home or no place of belonging. The chapter adroitly reveals different layers of resistance at many junctures as well as in the characteristics of many people.

The eighth chapter - *Re-inscribing the Cultural Ambit* - interrogate how the author offers a critique on the elite castes, their cultural discourses that has reduced the Dalit to a 'precarious other'. It analyses how the socio-cultural marginality of Dalits are represented in the book in order to effect a re-inscription of Dalit cultural ambit. The Dalits as outcastes were treated as contemptible, denied their fundamental rights and exploited by dominant castes. Dalits cultural oppression was far more dehumanising than their economic exploitation. Through their cultural representations, the dominant castes strove to achieve the agenda of reproducing the ideology of caste, of interpreting the identities of the oppressed and of constructing their stereotypical images. This chapter offers to counter this epistemological violence by deconstructing the stereotypical representations of the Dalits in 'Dalitist' (Dalit+elitist) representations and by constructing an alternative discourse.

This book is a fresh reading where readers are sure to enrich their knowledge and understanding about a Dalit life and its challenges in modern times. It further explores the covert possibilities which perpetrate the spirit of humanity through its well researched chapters.

- Dr. Praveen Kumar Anshuman, Ravi Prakash Chaubey

Chapter-1

Exploring the Leitmotifs of Food

- Deepna Rao

Introduction

Sharankumar Limbale's work *Akkarmashi*, translated as *The Outcaste* by Santosh Bhoomkar, presents us with the life of a man caught up in the cross-currents of the caste system in Maharashtra, India. As the illegitimate son of an upper-caste Lingayat Brahmin and a Mahar woman, he belongs to neither caste, and is therefore – as the title states, an 'outcaste'. A leitmotif is a recurrent, dominant pattern in a given work, which serves to outline a theme, or subtext in the given work. References to food, or the lack thereof, as well as passages dealing with hunger and starvation abound in Sharankamar Limabale's autobiography *The Outcaste*. While these serve to outline the privation and deplorable condition of the Dalit community of the Mahars, these passages also highlight numerous subtexts related to relations between people or family members, and sub-themes such as the lack of occupational opportunities, exclusion and changing social relations. Gastro-criticism, a form of literary criticism that deals with food and literature, as a field of critical discourse has often been applied to the field of cultural studies, but rarely in the domain of subaltern studies, much less Dalit Writings. Through this chapter, one would gain a fresh insight into the thematic aspects of Limbale's autobiography. Further, it can be argued that the experiences related to hunger and memories related to food are defining experiences for Dalit identity formation, both for the narrator and the community. Therefore, exploring these leitmotifs would prove fruitful in better understanding the nuances and layers of the text.

Understanding the Dalit Aesthetic and the Projection of Hunger

Limbale defines Dalit Literature in his book *Towards an Aesthetic of Dalit Literature: History, Controversies and Considerations*, as 'precisely that literature which artistically portrays the sorrows, tribulations, slavery, degradation, ridicule and poverty endured by the Dalits. This literature is but a lofty image of grief (Limbale, 2016: 30).' Indeed, hunger becomes a focal point at several junctures in the author's life narrative, which leads him to muse upon other aspects of grief. Food, a basic human right and survival need, eludes the Mahar community in this autobiographical novel. The starvation and angst that ensue become not simply a way of life, but metaphors of the deprivation and denial in other aspects of life. These leitmotifs are thus part of the Dalit aesthetic of the novel. The Dalit aesthetic in literature does not usually focus on beauty and pleasurable imagery and symbolism, but on the lived experience of Dalit life. This lived experience might find material expression even in images of starvation, or food that is left-over, scavenged or mingled with cow dung. Indeed, Alok Mukherjee has observed, 'Dalit (auto) biographical and fictional narratives and poetry neither hide nor romanticize anything (Mukherjee, A. In Limbale, 2016: 13).' Limbale himself has explained the Dalit aesthetic as not being concerned with simply beauty and pleasure, the universal values of art – but instead, with social values that determine the basis of the revolutionary ideals of the Dalit community. The Dalit aesthetic involves representing 'three values of life – equality, freedom and solidarity (Limbale, 2016: 120),' which constitute 'the essence of beauty in Dalit literature (Limbale, 2016: 120).' With a denial of basic rights such as food, and the social dignity of human existence, such literature then, explores different concerns from those motivated by the conventional artistic aesthetic, and one must examine these leitmotifs keeping in mind the uniqueness and motivations of the Dalit aesthetic.

Food, Shame and Solidarity in the Mahar Community: The Personal and the Universal

The leitmotifs of hunger, food and eating throw light on the solidarity in the Mahar community as well as the community's ostracized status in society. This is seen from the outset of the novel. The novel begins with the narrator's memory of a school picnic where he and

                                    The Famished Gods

his Mahar friends sat under a somewhat weather-beaten tree, away from the rest of their classmates. The reader initially discovers that the Mahar boys are not even aware that there is a picnic and have therefore not carried any tiffin, and have to rush home to bring along *jowar bhakari* and chutney.

Of the four boys, Parshya has no cloth to tie his *bhakari* in, while Umbrya has no chutney to accompany his *bhakari*. These are indicators of their poverty and inability to afford even a full meal. A regular Indian meal would comprise of some form of bread like a wheat roti or chappati, or a *bhakari* made of some form of millet grain. Chutney is usually an accompaniment. Lentils or dal, and some kind of cooked vegetables are other staples. The obvious absence of these staple items points to the deprivation and by extension the malnourishment of the boys. In addition, while it is not explicitly stated, their poverty is also inferred. The four boys can simply look on and smell the food of their classmates – and note that some even have fried food. Some high-caste girls, as the narrator notes, 'offered us their curry and *bhakaris* without touching us. The thought that they might have seen our food upset me. I was ashamed of my food and felt guilty eating it (Limbale, 2008: 3).'

Not only does one evince the socio-economic differences between the food of the high-caste students and the Dalit Mahar boys, but also the untouchability and segregation they must suffer during the picnic recess. The shame and guilt that the narrator experiences due to peer pressure and his societal position is also portrayed, without any kind of melodrama or sentimentalism. Yet, disturbingly, one also evinces that guilt and shame related to one's food is experienced by Sharan, the narrator-protagonist. The state of the food is such that it cannot be shared by the more privileged, an indirect testament to the poor quality and inedibility of the food.

Nevertheless, the higher-caste children do share their food, albeit leftovers. The leftovers are collected in a piece of paper and given to the Mahar children, and the group of four boys rushes to Girmallya's farm to eat them. The bundle of leftovers 'contained crumbs of different kinds of food and their spicy smell filled the air (Limbale, 2008: 3).' The narrator confesses that they 'had never tasted food like that before. We were all really gluttonous. Our stomachs were as greedy as a beggar's sack (Limbale, 2008: 3).'

Even if the leftover food consists mainly of 'crumbs' as opposed to complete food items in entirety, the narrator and his friends are greatly pleased with it and eat it heartily. Yet, the image of the 'beggar's sack' as a point of comparison with the stomachs of the boys makes one realize that the Dalit children were literally like beggars who had not begged, feeding off leftovers like scavengers.

Another point that the narrator remembers is how his mother Masamai would angrily shout, "What is it you have, a stomach or an Akkalkot? There seems to be a gizzard in your stomach. Why don't you go around with a big bowl at your mouth? (Limbale, 2008: 2-3)" The narrator compares his stomach to a 'graveyard' (Limbale, 2008: 2) and also recalls how upset his mother is with him after his return from the picnic. She wishes he had brought home some food for her as well, as she avers, "Leftover food is like nectar (Limbale, 2008: 3)." One realizes, through the episode, that it is not simply the children who live a life of malnourishment and hunger, but also their parents – and in this case, the narrator's mother. The comparison with both the graveyard and 'Akkalkot', the 'Samadhi' or renunciation spot for Swami Samarth, considered a re-incarnation of Lord Dattatreya (a Hindu deity), serve to show perhaps how hunger, a perennial truth and lived reality of the narrator's boyhood, must find its end – not in satiety – but in the stomach itself.

The mother, with a similar religious reference to 'nectar', associated with the Gods, while talking of leftover food, shows how leftovers are prized among Dalit people due to their deprivation and basic lack of food. The same comparison is evoked again, later in the novel, when Vani, Nagi and Nirmi develop a habit of stealing food every Wednesday, at the weekly market. Once, one of the sisters, Vani, is hit by a chappal or slipper for stealing a mere banana. The narrator muses, 'The poor steal for the sake of hunger. If they had enough to eat would they steal? Black-marketeers become leaders, whereas those who are driven to steal by hunger are considered criminals (Limbale, 2008: 21).' While the writer-narrator is not defending or justifying the crime directly, he displays a rational view of the crimes of Dalits. Crime is not seen to be motivated by any kind of personal greed but deprivation and starvation arising from sheer poverty – a social state of poverty neglected by society at large as a persistent social problem requiring attention and empathy. Often in the narrative, the personal shifts to the general, as the issues faced by the narrator-writer and his family members are not family or person-specific but plaguing the entire Mahar Dalit community. This universalized yet introspective vision might appear a paradox but is distinct to the Dalit aesthetic, as it enables the writer to deal with the larger social issues that require reflection on the part of the reader. Alok Mukherjee has written, 'the mimetic representation that Dalit literature is concerned with is not that of the life of the individual but of the community. (...) The events and experiences that this character [Sharan] narrates are real in that they actually happened, though not necessarily to the narrator. By making them part of Sharan's authentic experience, Limbale seems to suggest that each Dalit person's life partakes of the lives of all Dalits (Mukherjee, A. In Limbale, 2016: 12).'

The narrator himself confesses to having stolen a *bhakari* once from a friend, Nili. Nili's mother, Hausamai, would leave behind half a *bhakari* for her to eat through the day whenever she was hungry. One day, when Nili goes out to play, the narrator sneaks into her home to eat it. He confesses that he still recalls, to the present day, how the girl was restless throughout the day and weeping. Following the memory of this incident, we have one of the most philosophical and introspective passages within the novel:

Bhakari is as large as man. It is as vast as the sky, and bright like the sun. Hunger is more vast than the seven circles of hell. Man is only as big as a *bhakari*, and only as big as his hunger. Hunger is more powerful than man. A single stomach is like the whole earth. Hunger seems no bigger than your open palm, but it can swallow the whole world and let out a belch. There would have been no wars if there were no hunger. What about stealing and fighting? If there was no hunger what would have happened to sin and virtue, heaven and hell, this creation of God? If there was no hunger how could a country, its borders, citizens, parliament, Constitution come into being? The world is born from a stomach, so also the links between mother and father, sister and brother (Limbale, 2008: 50 – 51).

The *bhakari* becomes a symbol not simply for food, but the universe itself. Man is reduced to his state of hunger, and at the most primitive level, is no more than what his hunger is, and what he can feed himself. Whether one considers wars and crimes, or nation building, or even belief in God, the nascent strands lie in the hunger of people, in desire. The stomach is compared to earth itself, indicating how all is immaterial before human want and desire – a basic human need. Nothing holds value apart from satiating that hunger. The objects of desire may differ from one man's hunger to another, but ultimately, the entire world depends on the satiation of this need. Limbale thus, by universalizing hunger, presents the universal link between all people. Dalits are not alone in their hunger. All humans are guilty of instigating or mutely witnessing crimes that arose of hunger – and in certain cases, these crimes were of a greater seriousness, causing loss of life and the destruction of civilization. How then, can one castigate the Dalit community, and moreover children, who are victims of starvation and social neglect? Thus, one views both the personal and the universal through the image of the *bhakari*.

Food and Familial Relationships

The *bhakari* is also seen to depict the relationships between family members in Sharan's family, and throws light on the characters through incidents revolving around it. One such notable character is Santamai, the narrator's maternal grandmother. The narrator describes numerous incidents surrounding Santamai in the novel, and quite a few of these are involved with food and cooking. One memory of the narrator revolves around the collection of dung cakes and heaps. The narrator recalls how, during the harvest season, cattle would pass undigested grains of *jowar* through their dung. Santamai would separate these, wash these in the river, then dry them in the sun and grind them into flour. She would herself eat *bhakaris* made of this flour, while providing Sharan with *bhakaris* from the flour of regular, clean grains. Sharan, the narrator, recalls how he once tried to eat Santamai's *bhakari* and finding that it nauseatingly tasted completely of cow dung. But his grandmother would daily eat simply this, and never let her grandson siffer either the indignity of eating unclean grain, nor let him go hungry without *bhakari* if she could help it. The difference in the two flours displays, on the one hand, how Dalit women like Santamai would economize every grain, recognizing its preciousness, while simultaneously seeking to provide for their loved ones. They would suffer with the unhygienic, nauseating food but not allow family members and children to suffer similarly. Santamai, as a representative Dalit woman, through her actions, depicts the familial love and spirit of sacrifice that Dalit women display. The two different *bhakaris* here are markers then, of how, despite scarcity of food and resources, women would go through self-suffering but not shun their responsibility as providers. The dung-gathering activity too, is a demeaning activity that the Dalit community has endured for centuries and the scavenging of grain, by extension, is testimony to their impoverished social conditions, where grain was an expensive and elusive commodity, albeit an essential food staple.

In other incidents in the novel, the importance of fulfilling roles as guardians and providers is seen markedly, both on the part of Santamai, and Dada – the Muslim surrogate grandfather of the narrator. In the event there is scarcity of food, even scarce food items available are shared, or the adults go hungry for the sale of the children. While the family lives at the bus stand, they depend on Dada's earnings as a porter. Whenever he is given tea, he shares it with Sharan, and if given only half a cup, he gives it to Santamai. Yet, on some days, there would be almost nothing to eat. The narrator recounts:

> Most of the time, we went hungry. Sometimes there was only one bhakari in the basket. How could this one bhakari be enough for me, Dada and Santamai? Santamai's face would then look as if she was staring at a graveyard. She made me eat and went hungry herself. She made me eat and went hungry herself. I was the cause of the worry on such days. I would give just water to my hungry Dada. He drank it as if he were pouring water in the radiator of a bus (Limbale, 2008: 41).

Clearly, the major issue for the family of the narrator on several days is ensuring subsistence, and feeding the hunger of the children, not necessarily looking after one. The selflessness of both the elders is evident and the hand-to-mouth existence of the community is highlighted. Responsibility is placed before one's own subsistence and survival. Even the young narrator is conscious that he is the source of worry and anxiety to his elders. Although Dada is a Muslim and not a Mahar, his choice to live with a Mahar woman and adopt her family as his own subjects him to much of the same conditions that this Dalit community faces. Water, tea and tobacco are seen as items that quell the intense hunger experienced by people. There are passages that describe the process of liquor making and the hut where the children live with Masamai is converted to a drinking den. Yet, this bootlegging is not a profession of actual choice, but an exigency arising out of poverty. It is not as if Masamai wishes her children, mother and surrogate father to live at a bus stand. But she has to fulfil her responsibilities towards all her children. Similarly, the substance abuse of the adults is seen to arise from an acute need to blunt the pangs of hunger, and perhaps the depression arising from such trying, bleak circumstances.

In the latter part of the novel, when Sharan returns to the bus stand after going to college, Santamai makes egg curry especially for him, even after confessing that Dada has been spending all his money on liquor while she has to starve. In the same time period, when Sharan is called back to the village during the week-long Vithoba festival, and he goes with his friends, he is acutely aware of the poverty in which his family lives. When his friends leave, he finds that there is only one *bhakari* left over from the previous day, and it would not be sufficient for him, Santamai and Dada. Santamai, however, shakes the tin and says there is enough flour to make new ones and asks Sharan to eat it. Later, when she is away, Sharan curiously opens the tin, only to find that his grandmother has placed a heavy stone there as a ruse, to convince him that there is flour and that the elders will not starve. Both incidents display the love of the grandmother for her grandson, and the manner whereby she ensures Sharan is well-looked after, despite her own poverty, starvation and age.

While the adults look after the children well after the latter reach adulthood, sharing and consideration towards others is encouraged within the community. When Sharan returns from the picnic, for instance, at the start of the novel, his mother Masamai upbraids him for not carrying back some leftover food for her. He therefore tries to take some *kheer* home for his mother after a wedding feast in the village, but is thwarted by Girmallya. Girmallya's behaviour, too, is revealing, as it depicts how wasteful the higher castes are with food. Sharan is scolded by Masamai both for not bringing back *kheer* and for being too proud to go to the village just to eat at a wedding feast. Sharing, for the community, is an important

The Famished Gods

value and means of caring for others. A failure to do so results in a scolding. Similarly, one of Sharan's sisters, Nirmi, is scolded by the Mahar elderly women as she eats anything nice given by way of alms immediately instead of sharing with all in the family.

Dalit Starvation, Eating Habits and (So-called) Upper-caste Societal Attitudes

Santamai also begs for alms at a certain stage in the novel and is usually given food by various homes, a testimony to the fact that the social community ignores but is not ignorant about the hunger and starvation of the Mahar community. The narrator notes: 'At some houses she received flour; at others they gave her *bhakaris*. Soon her basket would be full of eatables. In the small container for oil some people would put coins (Limbale, 2008: 52).' That people dispense with food readily is an indication that they were aware of the need for food. Yet one does not see any offer of work, or any substantial help given either to Santamai or others. The narrator also mentions the importance of Dasera to the collection of food. On that particular day, 'The basket of a Mang enjoys some prestige (Limbale, 2008: 52).' Through this particular instance then, one witnesses the inconsistencies in Hindu society, where generosity is displayed only during festivals, to perhaps incur the beneficence of the deities, but not necessarily out of any goodwill or kindness.

Another inconsistency in upper-caste Hindus evinced is the tendency towards the holy animal, the cow. While the cow is revered in its lifetime, upon its death, the Mahar is left to tend to it and there is no further care shown towards the animal. Scavenging such animals becomes not simply a source of livelihood for the Mahar community members, the dead animals meat becomes a source of food for them. The narrator, Sharan, recalls, 'In a month when many animals died, we had enough to appease our hunger. But a month in which no animals died passed with difficulty, like the intercalary month. At such times, an animal was usually poisoned to death. Mankunna and Pralhadbaap went to a distant village to steal a buffalo and we spent the whole night slaughtering and cutting up the animal. In the morning, meat was cooked in every house (Limbale, 2008: 14).' Stealing and poisoning are once again brought up, but what is highlighted is the lack of occupation and employment as well. The Dalit community resorts to these acts of theft and slaughter of animals due to their sheer poverty and starvation, and a single dead animal serves to appease the hunger of the entire community.

The Mahar community boys are seen to eat not simply beef and buffalo meat, but also insects and other fauna that upper-castes might otherwise view disapprovingly. The narrator reveals:

> We used to roam along the stream to reduce the fire of hunger in our stomachs. We caught crabs, fish, eggs, smashed a honeycomb, caught birds, cried like water-fowls, tied frogs around our necks, searched for lizards, shot pebbles at kites with catapults, roasted squirrels and ate them. We went to the fields and felled the leaves and fruits from trees. We broke the ant-hill and ate the queen ant (Limbale, 2008: 65).

It would appear that Sharan, Harya and Parshya all eat whatever fauna meat that they can devour. In the absence of cultivated food like proper grain, vegetables and lentils, they have to rely on meat like hunters as this is available freely in the natural world. Nature becomes the provider to the poor, as there is none to provide for them, unless they beg. It also appears that even unpleasant tasks such as breaking an ant-hill or a honeycomb are also not beyond these youths, as their hunger guides them through the danger. They are so driven by danger; they do not care for danger or even convention – even if it is certainly unconventional to eat insects. Sharan, now at a more mature but nevertheless impressionable age, observes nature and sees the similarities between the pig who eats its own piglet and Devki, the woman who performed abortions, as well as Shankar, a drunken rascal who commits incest and impregnates his own daughter. Through the commentary and observations then, one also learns of the dark side of sexuality that Dalit women become victims of: some are simply sexually exploited, while others become the victims of incest – both equally reprehensible and in fact criminal acts legally.

The Attitudes of Mahar Children towards Animals, Dead animals and Meat

When younger, the Mahar children, including Sharan, are generally excited by the sight of a dead animal. Even one of the games they play involves enacting a dead animal and vultures. One child would pretend to be the dead animal while ten to twelve other children would pretend to be vultures. The role play of the children depicts the unusual attitude they have towards dead animals by virtue of their caste and the work and food that come to them by virtue of their caste. The dead animal doesn't signify death, decay or rot, nor is it something reprehensible. Instead, the children are seen to be quite unaffected by the reality of death in nature. Generally children are protected from the harsh reality of death but these children don't simply accept it, they are able to even weave imaginative role-plays and games around their observation of a dead animal and the vultures that scavenge the meat. Their excitement regarding the dead animal probably derives from the knowledge that they will get a full meal for several days and that every part of the animal is precious either in terms of food, or in terms of the hide that can be sold, and in terms of getting people employment for disposing of the animal.

The hunting activities of Sharan and his friends, as well as the children's role-play of the dead animal and vultures, point to the differential mind set of Dalit children compared to the higher castes. The poverty and starvation faced by these children shapes their mentality about animals and nature very differently. While they are sensitive and even knowledgeable about nature, nature and its realities manifest themselves differently to these children as they view the course of nature with a sense of detachment and predestination. They become hunters and scavengers of meat as there is no other form of ensuring survival and they accept these roles as life skills and as endemic to their lot.

Simultaneously, one witnesses through the character of Chandamai, Santamai's sister, that animals can even be loved dearly as pets and be well-looked after despite poverty. The animals don't always serve as meat – they serve as companions as well. Their food, however, can be a source of conflict. Chandamai's pet cat often ate up the chicken and fowl of the house, following which Masamai would ask Chandamai to tie the cat the house. When the children are asked to leave the cat on the other side of the river one day, Chandamai warns that killing a cat would be a sin. Days later, Chandamai is still gloomy and cheers up only when she adopts a kitten. Thus, one can see through the instance of Chandamai that Dalits are not necessarily cruel to animals, even if they are meat eaters, and forced by poverty to poison animals and hunt from time to time.

Food as a Marker of Caste

Later in the novel, when the narrator Sharan is avoiding inter-caste conflicts and violence against Dalits by taking refuge with his upper-caste surname, and living among Lingayat Brahmins, he in fact avoids eating meat. When Santamai and Dada visit him, bringing meat, they eat the meat at night. The need for self-protection takes precedence over dietary habits. Indeed, it is one of the few instances in the novel where the narrator is seen to hide his Dalit status and even worry about his grandmother and surrogate grandfather as being identified as coming from the *Maharwada*. Food thus plays a role as a caste marker as well.

The Caste Council and Food Provision

The role of the Caste Council is also highlighted in the manner whereby it provides employment contracts and food grain to the people of the Mahar community. The Caste Council provides its members with contracts for work at a specific time of the year, every year – on Pola day. Usually, these jobs were contracted and paid with grain in return. The entire *Maharwada* would gather in the community hall on the occasion and the Council would ensure that every family got a chance by rotation to earn food grain by this barter scheme. The jobs involved smearing the community hall with dung paste, lighting the street lamps at night and skinning dead animals. Thus, even the Caste Council had an important role in ensuring the livelihood and food supply of the community.

Yet, the Caste Council works in a manner that is within the norms of Casteism. None of the works offered are contrary to the modes of employment among Mahars. However, an incident in the novel with a tea-vendor Shivram is indicative of how an argument over tea and the practice of Untouchability can spark off revolutionary zeal for the cause of Dalit dignity. Shivram keeps a separate cup for Dalits to drink from. None of the Mahars object to the practice for several decades, as he offers them free tea for labour and this is appreciated by them. But the educated narrator and his friend Parshya decide to take the matter to the police-station. At first, even the police constable, who drinks tea on credit at the tea stall, doesn't

The Famished Gods

co-operate and threatens to place the two youths in jail. However, they are adamant and threaten to write to the Prime Minister. Finally, they are allowed to have their way, even if the village elders are highly upset with their actions. The incident displays how, well after the establishment of the Constitution, Untouchability was still practiced in India, and that even a minor rebellion was disapproved of. Yet, the incident is significant, as it displays the role of education and growing awareness and restlessness among the Dalit youth.

Conclusion

Thus, through all the incidents outlined above, one might conclude that the leitmotifs of food and hunger are indeed evocative not simply of the larger, dominant themes, they also throw light upon changing scenarios within the novel, and the relationships between characters. They present the solidarity among Dalits, as well as their segregation from the higher castes. Their poverty, lack of employment opportunities, deplorable living conditions, and need for a new, more just and egalitarian society are all highlighted directly or indirectly through incidents revolving around food and drink. The hunger for food and subsistence transmutes to a hunger for revolution, which may be seen as presenting the ultimate objective of Dalit literature. Limbale, in an interview with Mahuya Bhaumik, has asserted:

> My childhood is a mirror of my community and provides a reference point to all Dalits so that they can revolt against this torturous life, get united and achieve independence and democracy. My childhood is also a message to upper castes that by exploiting the Dalits they are exploiting majority of the population and thus not only depriving us, but also causing harm to the nation. It is a national damage that the upper castes are causing by exploiting us and by not providing us with proper opportunity (Limbale. In Bhaumik, 2017: 3).

Limbale's words resonate through the depictions in the novel and while the novel abounds with multiple disturbing images in line with the Dalit aesthetic, it would be fruitful to also pay attention to the images of starvation, hunger and meagre food, to gain perspective about the wider issues that plague the Mahar community and inform Dalit writings at large.

❑

Chapter-2

Inscription of Casteism through Stomach

- Surina Mol R.

Introduction

Sharankumar Limbale's *The Outcaste* is a real life narrative which addresses the malignant system of casteism in Indian society in a bildungsroman fashion. The different memories of Sharan that traverses through his family, village and wider social platforms, driven by Dalit activism expose the structural foundations of casteism like occupation, religion and food. Tracing out the different metaphors of food which makes it possible to narrate the memories and histories of the marginalized community, it is connected to the domestic and public realms; consequently the personal memories of food get a political dimension here. The food practices in his community are a confused category that etches the difficulty of existence of a Dalit whose lineage is fraught with chaos. Hunger is the reality and the food choices of the community arose because of the necessity of survival in a society where the economical and social privileges favour the upper caste. Consequently, meat eating and non vegetarian diet were seen as pollution. The fear of pollution crept in to the various sub castes inside the untouchables thus finalizing the varna system in Hindu society. The purity/ impurity division deconstructs food as a material category and makes us aware of its scarcity, deprivation, the tradition of storing and preserving food, the ways of finding and serving food etc. Food also becomes a site where gender intersections are also played. The perception of food by women, men and upper castes are also given thrust. Food is also a site of resistance and revolution where the explicit and implicit inscription of casteism is foregrounded.

Food and the Dalit Existential Dilemma

Food is the basic reality of our everyday life. It materializes the existence of an individual, community, and nation. The act of eating represents the different types of relationship and also decides who participates in forging a national identity through the food culture. Limbale stresses this aspect in his autobiography. "What about stealing and fighting? If there was no hunger how a country, its borders, citizens could, parliament, constitution come into being? The world is born from a stomach, so also the links between mother and father, sister and brother (50)." Limbale's personal narrative is a political statement, where hunger and the food choices forced upon on a community draws up the practice of casteist discrimination. Hunger is the everyday reality and 'food' is the issue of existence in Dalit communities.

The Outcaste is the autobiography of the author which traces the trajectory of a Dalit boy's growth from childhood to adulthood fighting against the evils of caste system. It narrates the difficulty of existence in a society where there is a lot of chaos created by caste. The predicament of numerous confusions of being born as an untouchable is described as follows: "How can I be a high caste when my mother is untouchable? If I am untouchable, what about my father who is a high caste? I am like Jarasandh. Half of me belongs to the village, whereas the other half is excommunicated? Who am I? To whom is my umbilical cord connected? (39)"

The quest brings him in connection with his village, the boundaries, the Women in his household, Dada, father, friends and finally to Dalit Activism. The story of food travels through these different phases exposing the different metaphors of food with respect to Dalit memories and histories. Food appears not as an independent category of choice but as a means of survival in a society where the laws, social and economic circumstances are set by upper caste people. Rege (2009) opines that food practices in Dalit communities appear as an invisibilised site of contentions, where numerous silent battles are raised to say 'I exist' (65). The problematic existence of a dalit creates bewilderment in his social interventions. The history of food is fraught with this dilemma. The crisis of identity and finding meaning in life starts with food. There is an intimate relationship between existentialist philosophy in the novel and alimentary truth.

The autobiography begins with Sharan's childhood memories of humiliation. He remembers a picnic in his schooldays. The upper caste pupils sat with the teachers and they had nice foods unlike the Dalit students who ate rotten food. The leftover foods were gorged greedily by them. The personal observation marks that food is central to the sustenance of caste system. Later when Saran was asked to write an essay on picnic, he was totally helpless. He was bitterly scolded by the school master for not writing his experience. The ingestion of food interspersed with casteist markers can severely impact clarity of thinking which makes Sharan bewildered. It never promises the pleasures of exploration and discovery.

> You, son of a bitch, come on, start writing, You like eating an ox, don't you … I remembered the hands of high caste boys and girls offering us their leftovers, withered tree in whose shade we sat, the bundle of left overs, the question my mother had asked, and the teacher calling me a son of a bitch and a beef eater. How should I start writing the essay my teacher had asked for? (4)

The gastronomic interests are a grave concern in the society and hunger makes one enjoy indiscriminatingly what one is eating, even it is rotten one, so far it is edible. So there is no heightened enjoyment of the meal. The dalits are deprived of healthy appetite and they cannot ascertain sensitivity to the subtle nuances of the food. Santamai could eat the jowar collected from dung and Vani could eat banana skin. The gastronomic experience reflects the social preference where hunger is carefully engineered experience in a distraught society. The subjective experience of hunger and appetite is connected to the existential field of enquiry. Kristenson comes with the idea of "social appetite" through which the symbolic value of food is connected with social class and gender. Bourdieu has analyzed the bourgeois eating habit that is attached to gratification, order and luxury and the working class with natural and straight forward eating (Bourdieu, 1984). Dalit food habits, appetites, satiety etc are not orderly and well articulated like the upper caste people. There is a terrible lack of representation and strong individual agency that guides the gustatory experiences. The social appetite of the left over people cannot be clearly etched out which is still scrutinized by the upper caste people through many labels. There is a constant tension between different forces in monopolizing food by which a specific food practice commands respect and status while others are denigrated. Ichijo and Ranta in "Food, National Identity and Nationalism: From Everyday to Global Politics" views that there is a certain hegemony of specific class in deciding a "national cuisine", practising and asserting the nation through food culture. The repetition of the word "beef eater" throughout the novel and norms of purity/impurity division decides the clashes between different groups to form the dominant food culture of a community.

Food Practices and Purity/Impurity Debate

Food not only gives the legitimacy to childhood memories but also materializes the spatial practices of caste system. The dalits are in fact the left over people, terribly exploited and segregated. Poverty is the reality in their homes. Hunger is not only connected to lack of supplies but also to social rejection. Sharan's mother scolds him asking why he did not bring leftover food. Finally, the teacher stabilizes the hierarchy of the caste by calling in to question the food practices in Mahar society. The word Mahar itself means beef eater. This term reinforces their degraded status.

Untouchability is wholly subsumed in to the habit of meat eating. The upper caste food practices are celebrated unlike Dalits. There is a hierarchical conception of food. Food items like Kheer, Chapati and curry were celebrated. It was so nice to hear these names uttered in the weddings and the dalit children were overjoyed and satiated by simply listening to these names. But they were denigrated and felt low whenever their food choices were openly scrutinized by the upper caste people. There is the process of social exclusion that augments the distribution of food in the society. Thus food habits are not individual or private choices. It is connected to moral and social relations. There is an ethical need for the classification of food in to pure and impure divisions. Food sets up boundaries and the metaphors of food are not neutral but ridden with particular ideas and sensibilities.

When Sharan ate the ox's flesh, he was teased by the upper caste boy. Sharan felt that the ox was dashing against the insides of the stomach. Pushpesh Pant (as cited in Agarwal, 2016), the food historian notes that caste is ingrained in our taste buds and eating habits. "Food snobbery is a part of India and the foods that belong to upper castes has always been more celebrated. In a caste sensitive India, labeling your product a Brahmin one is a way to communicate that it boasts of the highest form of purity (para. 3)." Ranto and Ichijo opine that food induces "everyday nationalism" which reinforces the existing and dominant ideas of nationalism (n.p).

The notion of purity and impurity is reinforced through food. They were given food during weddings but were offered no water. This particular gesture is an example of the line dividing the untouchables from the upper castes that is fixed and inviolable. In the case of Mahar society the occupation (skinning of animals) and beef eating are considered reprehensible by the upper castes. The fear of pollution is not only limited to Brahmin caste but also to the untouchables who have maintained code of purity/impurity inside the community. Sharan was scolded by Santamai because he has drunk water from the place reserved for Mangs, who comes under the lower hierarchy than Mahars. Shah, A.M. (2010) underscores the casteism inside the dalit communities:

> Although the untouchables were impure vis-à-vis other castes, and some of them performed highly impure work as that of skinning dead animals...they were all concerned about purity/ impurity in their own life. It seems every Untouchable caste had its norms in this regard, a higher one having more sanskritized norms than the lower ones. As the process of sanskritization operated as much among the rest of the castes, and there was a continuous striving among them to achieve higher levels of purity. The fundamental point is that, despite the line separating the untouchables from the rest of the Hindu society, all Hindus shared the culture of purity/impurity and untouchability was an integral part of this culture (176).

The sight of a dead cow or ox is a moment of celebration for the Mahars. Sharan closely observes the anatomy of animal with a scientific curiosity and preserves the meat. His hands "smelt of the raw flesh" while eating it (15). When Sharan ate pork he felt some sort of disgust. Eating pork comes under the impurity norm and it brings fear of pollution among certain communities of untouchables. Sharan's description evokes the metaphor of disgust:

We were not allowed to enter our homes unless we had a bath after eating pork... I thought of how these pigs eat human shit, they run around when hit with a stone, they struggle and fight to save their lives, they die with their feet tied up, they are roasted, their eyes fall out when they are roasted. Then my mouth, teeth, throat, stomach, intestines, blood, my whole self nauseated me (66).

Beef eating is treated as impure by the upper castes and those who eat beef automatically become impure. The skinning of the dead cow brings image of heroic exploit but the pig hunt is a repulsive for Sharan. The altitudes of dalit culinary culture, food habits, the ways of serving and finding food lie in the interface between the purity and impurity debate.

The Many Layers and Memories of Dalit Cuisine

Poverty and Hunger are the decisive categories that occupies in the liminal space of the purity/pollution intersection. Food culture in the Maharwada depended on what was easily available in the community. Beef was in great demand. Food has come out of necessity that is hunger and not out of trial and error method as there was a little food. We would never find variety or the use of costly ingredients in their cuisine. Animal fat was used to fry the meat. Chillies, salt and onions were the ingredients added because of its availability that shows the dalit sense of deprivation. Chandamai's culinary skill signals the scarcity of food items:

Chandamai would select a few pieces of dry meat, cut them in to smaller pieces with a sickle and roast them on a hot pan which melted the fat in the meat, causing it to sizzle. Chandamai used to roast crumbs of stale bhakaris in the same pan, with a spoon, then taking the pan off the, flames, add salt and chilli...When there was no meat, Chandamai used to fry Bhakari in the fat she kept in a small clay pot whose mouth was sealed with a piece of cloth (17).

Deepa Balkistan Tak (as cited in Masoodi, 2016) defines the dalit cuisine as born in the economics of survival, using resourcefulness and ingenuity to extract the maximum from available resources. "Be it land, food, water or food, Dalits had no rights to anything. Food practices were never made out of choice but were the fall out of a lack of options (75)." Food in dalit communities highlighted scarcity and deprivation. It can be relishing and nauseating depending upon their grade of existence inside the communal and social hierarchy. It is connected to lack of hygiene and nutrition. It should be stored and preserved. It is monotonous like the unchanged reality of Dalit life. Good food is an accidental discovery like a tiffin box Sharan finds that was left accidently on the bus by its owner. Leftover food was treated as nectar. Appadurai (as cited in Rege, 2009) gives cultural analysis of cook books that display caste and class hierarchies. "Leftover food has been a sensitive category in traditional circumstances…it was equated with the risk of moral degeneration and contamination…the cook books never made reference to those who were driven by the violence of caste regime discovered ways of drying up and storing food (75)."

Along with the storage and preservation, serving of food entailed the deprivation. Food was served in aluminium vessels. Steel utensils were considered as luxury. Here is a description of Santamai's kitchen:

> We washed and cleaned liquor bottles to store edible oil and kerosene. Two clay pots and a stove made by arranging the stones were our important possessions in our new dwelling…One basket for bhakaris, one dented aluminium vessel, two aluminium plates, two aluminium cooking vessel, clay pots…Dada had brought one tile from somewhere on which Santamai made bhakaris, and the same tile was used to crush chillies for the chutney…sometimes there were dead cockroaches in the curry kept in the clay pot…We threw the cockroaches away and ate the curry (42-43).

The alimentary representations indicates the categorization of the social and in these icons and symbols there is sometime an overturning of the schemata of caste politics and also a building up of a new cuisine with its own idioms.

Food and Gender Intersections

Limbale's description of food is made acute through his perception. How one could eat stale food is an intriguing question. Food and the perception of food by the different people in a community is also a point to be investigated. The taste of beef smelt like raw flesh while the taste of pork was nauseating and polluting. Jowar collected from dead body is polluting. Gopal Guru describes that the perception of food is determined by certain cultural hierarchies both across and within the social groups, which then can lead to the conditions of humiliation (2009, 3). Bhakari is an important staple food in Dalit communities. Sharan was shocked when he tasted his grandmother's bhakari made from the seeds collected from the cattle dung. It was actually dung itself. Santamai belonged to the older generation of untouchable and has endured the worst. The old generation confirms her status to that of animal shit. The cruel reality is also found in Vani eating banana skin. Masamai dismissed it by saying "Let her eat worm and live (22)." She has got a grade slightly higher to that of Santamai. She becomes the animal itself. Saran washes the banana skin in the river and began to eat it when he saw his schoolmaster coming by his way and he suddenly dropped it into the river. Santamai and Vani, being women and uneducated, never care the gaze of casteism. They are helpless and consciously accept the status of animal. Sharan averts the schoolmaster's gaze which is casteist. The various types of food are chosen as metaphors for the different relationships among the characters reflecting the problem of "Self" which is materialized through the author and its relation with the "Other".

Sharan's perception of food in his community traverses through the world of females in his household. Food is a site where gender intersection is also played. Most of the females in Sharan's household would gulp water and go to sleep while Saran was provided with a little food. Chandamai would cook beef for Saran with nice delicacies. The best pieces of beef are given to male folks. The female other is bound up with the existential question of female bodies, food and nourishment. Gopal Guru in "Food as a Metaphor for Cultural Hierarchies" gives a reading of gender differences in relation with food:

> The unequal relationship of food in terms of gender in Dalit community is not to be understood as reading of masculinity in Western theories but the pattern of consumption of meat is more in favour of male than a female. The meat is cheap but the preference for beef is also to be understood in terms of developing a consuming body but more importantly feeding the earning body…It also involved consideration of nutrition (Guru, 2009, 16).

The image of the body and self is superior in the males compared to the females. Sharan is the only person in the family who gets education unlike his sisters who are illiterate and choose to sell their body for money. The male folks can exist in the divisions of food/health, food/society and food/biology and the females can only exist in the category of food/sex. There is no extended metaphor of food for the female experiences. As a result, the female body is conceptualized as a source of indulgence and a location of moral indifference while male body is rational and self disciplined. Sharan's voice is rational compared to his mother who is irrational and unstable.

Food determines utility of body in the context of Dalit life. It stabilizes patriarchal family culture. Women were not the earning section. Santamai would do odd jobs and get some jowar or food in return. Masamai's body is caught within the confusion of food, lust and procreation. Women went around begging alms and brought food. Masamai sold her body for bread. She is a woman "caught between bread and lust" (64). They are economically and educationally deprived, suffering from poor health and has limited access to livelihood. Limbale has a keen observation on the neglect, violence and sexual exploitation suffered by Dalit women. Inspite of all these things, they are prone to differential treatment in accessing food.

The Future of Food

However food is also the site of transformation and rebellion in a caste ridden society. Sharan's Dalit activism began with education. He and his friend challenged the age old tradition of drinking from separate cup and saucer for Mahars in Shivram's tea shop by informing it to the police station. Food gets new signifier other than hunger that is right to be treated with respect. There are many symbolic instances of breaking the law of upper caste Hindus shown as Dalit empowerment but the implicit caste politics of food is there in Indian scenario that is vividly represented in *Akkarmashi*. When Sharan got a government job, he was economically raised but the possibilities of wider socialization that one gets through education and job was closed. He had to masquerade his personality among the Lingayats who were upper castes, when living around them. He had to adopt a Brahmanical garb, adopt a vegetarian diet and was scared of eating meat.

The marginalization of non-vegetarian food in a vegetarian locality causes one to hide his caste and its secret consumption makes one to unite with the memories and histories of food practices and conjoining realities of a Dalit. Santamai brought meat when she came to visit Saran out of love. The cooking and the dining habit enliven the family union. When Saran found the dogs dragging the left over bones outside the home, he was scared and felt as "if those dogs were tearing pieces off me and eating me up (105)."

The action of meat eating entails punishment and shame when viewed from the upper caste gaze. The food practices are not confined to domestic sphere and it cements up caste boundaries and identities. The public flogging of dalits on the pretext of allegedly carrying meat is an explicit reference to untouchability. At the same time, the preference towards Vegetarian corners, Brahmanical culinary traditions and products instill a dangerous, implicit casteism that purposefully erases the lived memories and exploitation faced by Dalits in the race towards modernity led by Sankritization and globalization. Limbale's autobiography explicitly states the casteist metaphors of food and resists the demands of upper caste modernity by emphasizing casteism as a lived reality.

❏

Chapter-3

Hunger and Exploitation

- **Sonali Rode**

Autobiography has been a distinct part of literature and an important testing ground for critical controversies ranging from the ideas of authorship, selfhood, representation and the division between fact and fiction. Autobiographical writings can be traced back to Plato's time and have expressed itself in the form of a genre since Rousseau's 'Confessions' was written. Now it is a popular form in the West as well as in the East. The post colonial study includes the autobiographies of the Third and Fourth World writers, such as Afro-Americans, the Indian Dalits and all the other subaltern autobiographical narratives.

Autobiography is an important segment of Dalit literature. Dalit literature has emerged through Dalit movement in Maharashtra in the 1960's and later in other part of the country. Dalit autobiographies are significant sub-genre of Dalit literature. It unveils the wretchedness and miseries of the Dalit's life and experiences through firsthand accounts. Dalit confessions mostly invoke the painful experiences that the author has gone through in the caste based society. Dalit writers write about their experiences with authenticity rather than soaring in the world of imagination.

The emergence of Dalit autobiographies opens up a new dimension to the study of autobiography in Indian literature. Dalits are marginalized entities and were denied education for long time by the society infested with casteism and social hierarchy. After being educated, some of them took writing as a weapon for self assertion and as an act of protest. For Dalit's writing an autobiography is an act of protest. They used this genre to achieve a sense of identity and mobilize resistance against different forms of oppression.

The genre of autobiography has flourished as a post- capitalist literary emergence which is generally believed to have the aim to record an individual's achievements and attainments. But this act of recording one's self achievements is not applicable in Dalit autobiographies. Instead of celebrating one's Self, it narrates the experiences and sufferings of the whole community. As Dalits got educated and were exposed to Ambedkarite ideology they became aware of the necessity to evolve a sense of Dalit consciousness among themselves and realized the need to portray their battered conditions through their writings. In the process they try to attain power from below by reconstructing their identity and social history. The Dalit autobiography plays an important role in reconstructing the Dalit historiography in the post colonial context of Indian literature.

The location of self is an important subject for analyzing an autobiographical text. The identity of a person is determined on the basis of location to which he or she belongs. And the person undergoes the experiences likewise. In autobiographies all the aspects of the life ie political, social, economic, religious, psychological, philosophical etc.are considered in order to understand the narrator's life, time and society.

To the deconstructionist, the self image of stable identity that many of us have is really just a comforting self- delusion which we produce in collusion with our culture. We may say that culture itself is stable and coherent when in reality it is highly unstable and fragmented. As a matter of fact, we don't have identity as the word implies that we consist of one singular self, but in fact, we are multiple and fragmented, consisting at any moment of any number of conflicting beliefs, desires, fears, anxieties and intentions.

The Dalit autobiographies have penned their experiences of pain and sufferings at physical as well as psychological level. They suffered at various levels like social, economical, political and cultural through the processes of deprivation, caste segregation, untouchability, denial of education, abject poverty, forced child labor, exploitation of women, physical and mental persecution, de-humanization of their body and so on. These experiences made the Dalit autobiographers and their community to fight for their identity, respect and social emancipation through education and assertive articulations. In the Dalit autobiographies the writers have successfully recorded their experiences of oppressions and deprivation through their attempt to reconstruct their individual as well as social history. The Dalit autobiographies are formidable examples of subaltern narrative of self. Dalits were physically segregated from the main stream and this fact has been prominently expressed in their autobiographies.

Specific features of Dalit Autobiographies are as follows:
1. Most of the Dalit autobiographies are written in the early part of the author's life.
2. The identity assertion is one of the key features of Dalit autobiography with an emphasis on caste, class, gender, ethnicity, language, region, etc.
3. The Dalit autobiographies are largely recollections of their wretched experiences as social pariahs and veritable outsiders.
4. By defying the existing norms imposed by mainstream codes, the Dalit autobiographers mobilize resistance.
5. Through the writing of autobiographies the Dalit writers try to rediscover and reconstruct their socio-cultural history of dehumanizing oppression and exploitation in every sphere of life.

Writing an autobiography is a political act because there is always an assertion of the narrative self (Kumar, 3). Autobiography involves remembrances, but this act of remembrance is not a random act but a process of selective recollection. The location of self is an important subject for analyzing an autobiographical text. The identity of a person is determined on the basis of the location he belongs in the society because the person will undergo the experiences in life accordingly. There is a need to study the autobiography from different point of views like social, political, economic, psychological, religious, and philosophical in order to understand how the author coped up with his/her life, time and society.

Sharankumar Limbale has made use of his writings not merely to entertain his readers but to make them aware about the abject conditions of the lines of the members of their community who are exploited without any fault on their part. He has resisted the caste system as well as the poverty and humiliation which it brings. He has brought a larger stage for the depiction of the social, cultural and political process of marginalization.

Sharankumar Limbale in *The Outcaste* narrates the settlement of the untouchables in Marathwada. He tells us about the troubling experiences of untouchabilty that degenerated into social evil which has hugely affected education in schools, social transactions and relationships. The autobiography begins with the descriptions of how untouchability remained a strong and constant preoccupation among teachers and students of high caste even during the events like school picnics. He refers to the sitting arrangement of the students where high caste students were allowed to sit along with the teachers under a banyan tree while the Mahar students were asked to sit under another tree. He writes:

> Boys and girls from the higher caste like wani, bramhin, marwadi, muslim, Maratha, teli, fisherman, goldsmith and all the teachers, about hundred or so sat in a circle under the tree. We the Mahar boys and girls were asked to sit under another tree. The high caste ones said a prayer before eating, which didn't make any sense to us (2).

The Outcaste presents lots of incidents where the narrator was ill-treated in the school by his classmates and teachers as untouchable. During rainy season the school would move to Shivappa teli's mansion and sometimes to Marwari mansion the Mahar students were made to sit at the doorstep and not inside the room. Limbale could not understand the reason. He writes:

> There were so many caste factions in our school. The umbilical cord between our locality and the village had snapped. As if the village had cut it off like an unwanted part and thrown away. The untouchables grew up like aliens since their birth. This alienation increased over the years (5).

Limbale says that these awful memories still haunt him. Apart from the school he has to face the untouchability in his day to day social life. He saw that Brahmins used upstream of the river bank

The Famished Gods

for water and for washing clothes, the downstream was used by kunbis and shepherds; and the lowest stream was for Mahars. Other than this there are many instances of untouchability like barbaer's denial to cut narrator's hair, restrictions imposed upon them to take water from Narayan patil's well, etc. which illustrate the deeply rooted practice of untouchability that was so indignantly prevalent in society.

In this autobiography, Limbale keeps record of his past experiences and he lives those experiences again and again. These experiences are not fictitious but they are his memories. His writing style depicts his personality. All the experiences presented in the autobiography are experiences of the writer himself. The experiences which are engraved on his mind are reflected in *The Outcaste*. Sharankumar Limbale says that one has to be fearless and shameless while writing autobiography. It has hatred and love in it and that's why it is more alive than any other literary forms. Limbale also says that while writing autobiography he had only memories in his mind and he put them into words. He also says Dalit people feel that these autobiographies bring out the dark side of the society while high caste people consider it sensational.

During the month of Shravana when people read Holy Scriptures, Sharankumar and his friend Parshya went to the temple unnoticed by people. But Parshya's father scolded them:

> I want to live in the village. Why do you boys behave like this? The village will humiliate me some day because of your behavior. No one has ever had slandered me for anything. I'll break your leg if you behave like this again. He was really angry because entering temple is a crime. We were supposed to say our prayers from the steps outside. Our entering the temple will make god impure. We were expected to responsibly. The untouchables must not enter the temple (62).

This caste system is humiliating and discriminating. Sharankumar raises a question that whether it was really a god who made human beings to hate each other. We say that all are children of god then why do we discriminate. Why these low caste people are ill treated always. He also asks when every person's blood is red why high caste people keep dalits away from them:

What kind of god is this that makes human beings hate each other? We are all supposed to be children of god, then, why are we considered as untouchables? Why are we ostracized? Why are kept away from other human beings? Why are we kept out of own selves? Why is this discrimination between one human being and another? After all, isn't everybody's blood red? (62).

These questions try to uproot the superstitions about untouchability. The Mahars and Mang were not allowed to fetch water from the well which was dug by them. These incidents show how untouchability has become leprosy, a social stigma on society.

Limbale and his people living at the bottom of the social level experience rejection, subhuman treatment and suffering everywhere. The caste system is its root cause. It is contempt for human life. This system can be compared with the racial system of the white and blacks. What Dr. Martin Luther King, Jr. says about the struggle between the whites and blacks is also true about Indian caste system:

> It is arrogant assertion that one race is the center of the value and object of devotion. It is the absurd dogma that one race is responsible for all the progress of history and alone can assure the progress of the future. Racism is estrangement. It separates not only bodies, but minds and spirits. Inevitably it descends to inflicting spiritual or physical homicide upon the out group (70).

During his stay in Ahemadpur, Sharankumar was unable to get room. So, he has to hide his caste. He says he felt like an outsider and he was always worried what if his caste was revealed. In Latur too he met with same experience. Finally he had to go to Bhimnagr to live. His room was near cemetery where he has to bear smell of burning bodies. He says even though he brushed, bathed and wore clean clothes everyday yet he couldn't escape from his low caste status.

The Outcaste is more poetic than realistic as it bears the stamp of contemporary literature. Autobiography is reflection of life the one has lived, seen and experienced. Sharankumar Limbale says that after its publication he has to suffer a lot at the hands of his family as well as his community. While describing his school days, he tells

The Famished Gods

us about the school picnic he and his friends went to. During the picnic the higher caste students sat with the teachers and shared delicious food with each other. While Mahar students made a circle away from them and ate chutany bhakri. Even the games they played were very different. Brahmin students were playing kabaddi while Mahar students were catching each other. Their way of playing, eating, praying creates a valley of separation between higher caste and Mahar students. A very heart touching image is used by Sharankumar Limbale here for stomach. He says that our stomach is like a cemetery where infinite number of corpse could be burnt. As they never had enough food at home he had very less to eat. At the end of the picnic the higher caste students gave leftovers to these children and they ate the food like hungry vultures.

In the book, Sharankumar has described very touching images of hunger and how the lower caste people fight for a single morsel of food. Hunger is a monster for these people whose stomach can never be filled. He describes a wedding ceremony of upper caste. They had a grand feast for the viallge. The guests and villagers ate first and the Maharwada ate last if called or else they watched like dogs and accept humiliation for cursed stomach. During a wedding feast, he tried to sneak *kheer* for his mother Masamai and out of which occurred an insult in his life:

He snatched my plate full of kheer. Threw it on the ground and slapped in the face, 'son of a bitch', he shouted. If you don't want it why the hell did you take it? Don't let me see you more than one any feast after this feast. I returned home crying (9).

To fill the stomach was Llimbale's primary purpose. He wondered for food, killed animals, dug roots, cut fruits but was helpless. He says, "He started selling himself for stomach. A woman becomes whore and man a thief. The stomach makes you clean shit; it even makes you eat it (8)." He says during the wedding feast the Maharwada would be all ears waiting for invitation with eager stomach. Their stomach was ears, their stomach was pan. He felt that god has committed a mistake by giving man a stomach.

He and his grandmother Santamai used to collect cowdung and during the harvesting season they used to collect the dung which contained undigested grains of Jawar. Santamai used to wash the dung in the river and collect the grains. After drying up those grains she used to prepare bread (*bhakri*). Limbale says when he ate that bhakri it had smell of cowdung and he could not eat it. But santamai could eat if without any feelings like a machine. In all these and other aspects *The Outcaste* is a dreadful reflection of the society.

Sharankumar Limbale faced this evil throughout his life by eating dead beaf, dried roti-chhtuni and even abusese by the savarna community. His poverty made him suffer. Being member of a large family having no male support he faced lots of humiliation at the hands of higher class people. His search for food went thus:

> We used to roam along the stream to reduce the fire of hunger in our stomach. We caught crabs, fishes, eggs, smashed honey combs, tied frogs around our necks, searched lizards, shot pebbles at kites with catapults, roasted squirrels and ate them.we went to the field and fell the leaves and fruits from the trees. We broke the anthill and ate the queen ant- Umbreya, Parashya and I broke the trunks, particularly the tadi palm for their pith. We did all this to satisfy our hunger (65).

Other than hunger the problems Mahars faced were chiefly related to different layers of exploitation. Women in The Outcaste are Dalit of the Dalits. They have to suffer a lot because they are women. Gail Omvedt in an interview says, "Men are at the top and women are on the bottom like crushed and wasted powder. And at the very bottom are the dalits and below them are the suppressed dalit women (Gail, 321)."

Masamai, Chandamai and Santamai suffer a lot due to their inferior status in their own community. Women in Dalit community are victimized doubly, on the pretext of her lower caste status and as a woman. The woman characters in *The Outcaste* are widows, childless, deserted women, marriageable girls and hence a humiliated womanhood. Sharankumar Limbale doesn't show any dislike or dishonor to them. It shows his respect towards womanhood. Though his mother and grandmother had committed adultery, he understands in which circumstances they had done it and doesn't harm or blame them with words. His tone is neither angry nor sympathetic towards them. This silence is enough strong and talkative about his patience and protest.

His mother Masamai is a dominant character in the autobiography. She has to suffer a lot and live with tragic fruits of situation. Limbale writes about his mother in acknowledgement:

My mother is untouchable, while my father is a high caste from one of the privileged classes of India. Mother lives in a hut, father in a mansion. Father is a landlord; mother landless. I am an akkarmashi (half caste). I am condemned, branded illegitimate. I regard the immorality of my mother and father as a metaphor for rape. My father had privileges by virtue of his birth granted to him by the caste system. His relationship with my mother was respected by society, whereas my mother is untouchable and poor. Had she had been born into high caste or were she rich, would she have submitted to his appropriation of her? It is through the Dalit movement and the Dalit literature that I understood that my mother was not an adulterous but the victim of a social system. I grew restless whenever I read about a rape in the newspaper. A violation anywhere in the country, I feel, is violation of my mother (Introduction, IX).

Masamai was married to Ithal Kamble, a very poor man. There was always shortage food in her house. Itahl Kamble worked as a farm labor to a landlord Hanmanta Limbale, a Patil. He also helped Ithal in his hard times. But while helping him his intention was quite different. Hanmanta patil lured her out of her poverty and exploited her sexually. This ruined Ithal's family which was happy in its own way. After this the Jaat Panchayat forced her to divorce Ithal Kamble and she has to leave her children behind. She questions the society that a relationship can come to an end but a relationship between mother and her sons can never end.

Masamai's exploitation causes Sharankumar Limbale worry about his identity. His father is Lingayat and Mother is Mahar. A Muslim man, Mahmood Dastgir Jamadar called as Dada lives with his grandmother and in this sense his grandfather is a Muslim. Limbale says:

Does this mean I am Muslim as well? Then why can't the Jamadar's affection claim me as a Muslim? How can I be high caste when my mother is untouchable? If I am untouchable what about my father who is high caste? I am like Jarasandh. Half of me belongs to the village whereas half is excommunicated. Who am I? To whom is my umbilical cord connected? (58).

After Hanmanta left Masami, Yeshwantrao Sidrappa another Lingayat Patil used her as a keep. She gave birth to Nirgi, Nirmi, Vani, Suni, Parmi, Shrikant, Indrya and Sidram, eight children from him. All men in Masamai's life exploited her and left her. She brought her children up with poverty and humiliation. As she became the victim of lust of upper castes, she was called as whore by patils. Limbale rightly points out that people who enjoy high caste privileges, authority sanctioned by religion and inherit property have exploited the Dalits of this land. The patils in every village have made whores to the wives of Dalits. A poor Dalit girl on attaining puberty has invariably been a victim of their lust. There is a whole breed born to adulterous patils. There are Dalit families that survive by pleasing the patil's sexuality.

Because Masamai delivered illegimate children it was impossible for her to think of any other life. She was unable to take care of them or provide them facilities. But it harms her son's sensitive mind. He tells us he never got real love from his mother, so she was not his mother in true sense. Half of her was his mother and other half a woman for patils. His mother never got status and position in her life either with Hanmanta or Yeshwantrao whom Sharankumar called Kaka. Whenever he came to his home he behaved like a father but the same man shut the door of his house when he saw Sharan lingering in fornt of his home.

Masamai's exploitation by the privileged masters is a record of the atrocities carried out by age old traditional social system. She symbolizes the women of her community. The Dalit women are twice victimized: by the husbands and by high caste people but they are defenseless. Masamai is excluded from all the comforts of life but the major tragedy of her life is that she is not allowed to enjoy any status in her family life with her children. She is just a thing to be used for the men. These men cannot accept their children and these children lead to illegitimate children's rootless lives. Masamai is an epitome of stoicism. Masamai's predicament underlines the need of granting human diginity to Dalit women and safeguarding the pious motherhood.

The Famished Gods

More than Masamai Sharan is attached to his grandmother Santamai. He says, "My mother, always treated me as if I was her stepson. I was more attached to Santamai, my grandmother. Whenever Masamai began to hit me Santamai would intervene and save me (42). Santamai is another humiliated character and illfated woman in Outcaste. Though widow she loves Mohmood Dastgir Jamadar. He has illicit relationship with her. He worked as a porter at bus stand. Though she is a Mahar and he a Muslim, hunger kept them together throughout the life. It was difficult for Saharankumar Limbale to explain their relationship to his friends and relatives.

After a quarrel between Masamai and Santamai, Santamai left his mother's home and began to live in the open behind the bus stand with Sharan and Dada. Santamai's struggle for food is implausible. She used to store bhakris in a wooden chest full of bugs and cockroaches. Sometimes there used to be dead cockroaches in clay pots of curry but they used to throw away cockroaches and ate the curry. Santamai used to clean the bus stand but no one respected her.

How to satisfy hunger was a great question for Sharankumar and his family. Once Limbale came hom from Solapur with some of his friends. Santamai cooked food for them. On the second day when his friends were gone Sharankumar was hungry, but he saw that there was only one bhakri left and he was extremely hungry. Santamai showed him a box saying that it has flour. So Sharan ate the bhakari and later discovered that there were stones in the box. This shows Santamai's love for Sharan and also her constant struggle for food. Like his mother Santamai too was not exempted from the lust of rich caste. When Sharan needed money for higher studies she took him to the money lender. The moneylender kept on looking at Santamai's breast peeping through her torn blouse and refuses to give money. Sharan says, "His looks spread like poison in my heart. I wished that the blouse of this moneylender's mother or sister was torn so that I could stare at their breasts. I burned within. Our poverty was detestable. I wanted to rebel against such humiliation (82)."

Women whether of Savkar's or Mahar's suffer the same fate at the hands of men. Even after having a wife Sidrappa had two keeps, Jani and Masami. They were sexually harassed. Dalit women had to bear it out of hunger and poverty. They were insulted due to untouchability. Negi, Limbale's sister loved and married Nandu, senior patil's son. She was sexually assaulted as her husband remarried another patil girl. This brought tragedy in Negi's life. About Negi, Santamai tells Sharankumar, "Negi has gone astray; she is going around with Nandu, the son of senior patil, these days (85)." thus we can see the suffering and sexual harassment of Mahar passed from generation to generation. Women are sex toys for the upper caste people. They have no social status and no consciousness which resulted into their suffering. Cheap life of women has been reflected in Outcaste and with this the author has exposed lusty brutal nature of higher caste people.

Throughout the autobiography we can also find the theme of quest for identity lingering. The author is on the journey of searching self identity. He finds out that due to caste system his identity is broken, shattered and unacceptable in the caste based society. In the introduction itself he raises the question of his identity. Having a low caste mother and high caste father makes him half caste ie not here not there. His identity is hung between. *The Outcaste* reflects social history of Indian society. It criticizes objectively the naked reality hidden behind the so called ideal curtains of Indian society. It exposes the pretentious mask of the morals and ethics of Hindu religion. Instead of remaining dumb and deaf, he has rebelled and revolted against the atrocities of upper society. He makes us think by raising questions of which we had never thought of. He does not write to gain sympathy but to soothe his burning soul that doesn't allow him to relax.

Sharankumar's father objects the use of his name in the school register. His father rejects and hence the upper caste rejects him.this rejection humiliates him and he has to undergo penetrating odds of life. Being Akkarmashi, he has to accept all the curse of untouchability. He was also worried about his fate in Dalit movement. His struggle signifies the persistence of the caste differentiations in the last quarter of the 20th century. The problems created by Masamai's motherhood make his struggle miserable for getting educational opportunities and social recognition. When Sharankumar applies for freeship in school he needs his form to be signed by his parents and sarpanch.

But the sarpanch refuses to sign because he does not like guardian's name Masamai Hanmanta Limbale.

Sharankumar Limbale in the second part of his autobiography, *Punha Akkarmashi* states:

...this is digging of a life; thousands of years' sorrow remained buried outskirts. This huge heap taken out is of injustice, poverty, insult and dreadful experiences of untouchability. Had I not dug out this heap an ancient truth would have remained hidden. This ancient truth is epitome of my self-respect incurved in Ambedkarite alphabets (Punha Akkarmashi, V).

Disgust of caste based culture and quest for identity made Limbale to walk on the path of revolt. During his college days he came to know about Ambedkarite philosophy and was influenced by it. It made him realize that his mother and he himself were not responsible for his humiliation but the system that governs the society. Chungi to Chapalgaon is the travel of Sharankumar Limbale for education. It was also his journey from darkness to light, humiliation to respect and ignorance to knowledge. He could shift towards Buddhism in Chapalgaon. At Solapur, while studying in Dayanand College, he felt free in the new environment. Here, he realized the hypocrisy of Lord Brahma and the scriptures related to him. He realized the falseness and came to know the reality. Education enlightened him. He raises questions with logic. "If one had enough, why would one steal? Why would one suffer at the hands of police? While studying in the college, I was mentally aflame (83)."

After this awareness, he stopped saying 'Namaskar' and started saying 'Jai Bhim'. He says, "I substituted Babasaheb for Ambedkar since it sounded less formal and most respectful. My youth has assumed a new meaning and significance (87)."

Sharankumar faced problem of identity. His fractured identity humiliated him a lot. He witnessed inhuman suffering in his life and strongly rejected Hindu caste system. He raised questions about his self respect. The Outcaste raises voice against poverty, hunger and humiliation of the poor people separated from the main stream of the Hindu religion. He also raises issue of exploitation of women, untouchability and caste conflicts. Sharankumar stands fro self respect, dignity and pride for those who suffered and have been suffering like him.

Sharankumar expresses the bitterness and deprivation in *The Outcaste*. Moreover, his book becomes a record of the cruelty of India's caste system. *The Outcaste* has out forth the dark life of the oppressed people. Limbale espouses change and transformation of the society in order to overcome the wrong beliefs and inequalities which fling humanity into perilous state affairs. He observes the social and political worlds through his insightful senses. Even after the independence the caste ridden India fails to terminate caste difference. Sharankumar Limbale wishes to amend the caste system and thinks of a system founded on humanity. His efforts have clear contemporary relevance, even considering the current dynamism of Indian social relationship.

❑

Chapter-4

A Tale of Ceaseless Atrocities

- Darshan Lal

Introduction

Dalit Literature is known as the 'literature of protest and anger'. The aim of Dalit Literature is to protest against the established Brahmanical system which was based on injustice and to expose the evil and hypocrisy of the high castes. With regard to this, Limable remarks: "Dalit Literature is unflinching in portraying the seamier side of Dalit life (Limbale, 2004, 13)." Dalit writers are expressing the exploitation and subjugation of the whole Dalit community through 'self-lived' experiences. In ancient times, Dalits were subjugated and exploited by the upper castes. They didn't have the right to get education. If any of the Dalits tried to resist, he was silenced by the so called upper castes. During Bhakti period, certain Bhakti Saints and gurus tried to abolish caste-discrimination. Guru Nanak Dev ji, Saint Kabir, Saint Ravidas, Tukaram tried their best to bring all the communities on a single platform. They tried to abolish caste-system and untouchability. During medieval period certain Sufi saints also tried to bring equality and fraternity through their teachings. Various social reformers like Periyar, Mahatma Jyotiba Phule and Dr. B.R. Ambedkar struggled very hard for the emancipation of the Dalits. It was only Dr. B.R. Ambedkar, who took a giant step for total liberation of the chains Dalits were imprisoned with. He fought for social equality that was based on democratic principles of liberty, equality and fraternity. Babasaheb gave the slogan, "Educate, Organise and Agitate." He said that education is the most powerful weapon for the liberation of the down-trodden. Through education one can bring social change.

The legacy of Dr. B.R. Ambedkar and Mahatma Jyotiba Phule has inspired many Dalit writers. All the Dalit writers have been influenced by Babasaheb's teachings and they are doing the most tedious task of documenting the exploitation and subjugation of the whole Dalit community through 'self-lived' experiences. Limbale writes: "It is not the pain of any one person, nor is it of just one day - it is the anguish of many thousands of people, experienced over thousands of years (Limbale, 2004, 31)." Regarding this R.G. Jadhav very aptly remarks: "Dalit writers are doing the difficult task of portraying this life, through personal experience and empathy, absorbing it from all sides in their sensibility. To live this life is painful enough; it can be equally painful to recreate it on the mental level (Jadhav, 2009, 310-311)."

Caste: An Unseen Ghost

Sharankumar Limbale in his autobiography has given a plethora of examples of injustice, sexual abuse, caste-discrimination, untouchability, lust, poverty, hunger, superstitions and resistance. Dalits' struggle for identity and against hunger and poverty run throughout the book. Dalits were forced to live in poverty by the upper castes because of their caste. Strategically Dalits were driven out of the pale of society by Manu and were exploited because of their caste and poverty. They were treated less than animals. About caste G.N. Devy in the Introduction of *The Outcaste* remarks: "Caste is a lived experience in India more than a prescribed mode of social classification (Devy, 2003, xiv)." Mr. Devy again remarks: "...caste as a status marker has probably been the most unique feature of Indian society (Devy, 2003, xiv)." Regarding this, Dr. B.R. Ambedkar remarks:

It is a pity that caste even today has its defenders. The defenders are many. It is defended on the ground that caste system is but another name for division of labour and if division of labour is a necessary feature of every civilized society then it is argued that there is nothing wrong in caste system....Caste system is not merely division of labour. *It is also division of labourers.* Civilized society undoubtedly needs division of labour. But in no civilized society is division of labour accompanied by this unnatural division of labourers into watertight compartments. Caste system is not merely a division of labour, which is quite different from division of labourers — it is a hierarchy in which the divisions of labourers are graded one above the other. ...Now the caste system will not allow Hindus to take to occupations where they are wanted if they do not belong to them by heredity. If a Hindu is seen to starve rather than to take new occupations not assigned to his caste, the reason is to be found in the caste system. By not permitting readjustment of occupations, caste becomes a direct cause of much of the unemployment we see in the country. As a form of division of labour the caste system suffers from another serious defect. The division of labour brought about by the caste system is not a division based on choice. Individual sentiment, individual preference has no place in it. It is based on the dogma of predestination (Ambedkar, 2007, 14-15).

Caste system is contempt for human life. This caste system may be compared with the racial struggle between blacks and whites. Comparing racial exploitation to caste system, King Jr. Martin Luther observes:

It is the arrogant assertion that one race is the centre of value and object of devotion. It is the absurd dogma that one race is responsible for all the progress of history and alone can assure the progress of the future. It separates not only bodies, but minds and spirits. Inevitably it descends to inflicting spiritual or physical homicide upon the out-group (Luther, 1967, 70).

Limbale was born and brought up in a casteist environment. Being an outcaste he was doubly exploited—being Dalit and being an outcaste. Limbale said in the Acknowledgements of *The Outcaste*:

My history is my mother's life; at the most my grandmother's. My ancestry doesn't go back any further. My mother is an untouchable, while my father is a high caste from one of the privileged classes of India. My mother lives in a hut, father in a mansion. Father is a landlord, mother landless. I am an *akkarmashi* (half-caste) I am condemned, branded illegitimate (Limbale, 2003, ix).

Sharankumar Limbale resists against this rotten system and has exposed the hypocrisies of the upper caste society thorough personal narrative. He tells that when he went to school for taking admission, the headmaster asked him the name of his father. Limbale didn't know who his father was and started attending the classes regularly. The headmaster Bhosale ironically called

Limbale, 'the Patil of Baslegaon' (45). This hurt Limbale's heart deeply. For taking admission in 8th standard Limbale had to take the sign of the Sarpanch of Chungi. But Sarpanch refused to sign and disapproved the name of his mother Masamai. Sharankumar felt that he was like an outsider, he "had neither a father's name, nor any religion, nor a caste... had no inherited identity at all (59)."

Sarpanch somehow signed the freeship form but whatever he said deeply hurt Limbale. Sarpanch says:

Can anyone guarantee that he is the offspring of the father whose name is added to his name? Has anyone seen who sowed his seed? Has anyone seen the intercourse of his parents that resulted in his birth? (59).

These comments of Sarpanch deeply pierced Limbale's soul and heart. This shows the inhuman treatment of the high-caste Sarpanch towards Dalits who had no identity and they had no right to live with dignity and honour. The exploiters always lived enjoyable and respectful lives while the exploited always became the victim of upper-castes.

Limbale wanted to study further after schooling. He went to borrow money from many persons, but got only humiliation and insults in turn. Seeing Limbale too curious for his studies, his grandmother Santamai decided to get him educated at any cost. She begged everyone for help but in vain. Limbale and his grandmother went to a moneylender for money. Limbale was shocked to see the conduct of moneylender. The moneylender was staring sheepishly like a vulture at the torn blouse of Santamai. Limbale has very rightly remarked:

Santamai and I went to a moneylender. He was drunk. Santamai and I stood at some distance from him. Santamai's blouse was torn exposing her breast. The moneylender kept staring at the peeping breast, but he refused to lend us the money. His look spread like poison in my heart. I wished that the blouse of this moneylender's mother or sister was torn so that I could stare at *their* breasts. I burned within. Our poverty was detestable. I wanted to rebel against such humiliation (82).

This shows the mean nature of upper caste men and Limbale's anger and feeling of protest against such base people. Limbale was very afraid because of his caste so he couldn't claim the name and caste of his father openly. In real sense, Limbale said that he was not a Mahar, "because high-caste blood ran in my body (82)."

Because of his birth and caste, Limbale faced humiliation wherever he went. He was so broken that he seemed himself like an alien on this land. He remarks: "I am an alien. My father is not a Mahar by caste. In the Maharwada I felt humiliated as I was considered bastard; they called me akkarmashi. Yet in the village I was considered Mahar and teased as the offspring of one (62)." He again remarks: "My father lives in a mansion, my mother in a hut, and I on the street. Where will I die? Where are my roots exactly? (62)" This shows the plight of a Dalit boy. Same is the case in Bama's *Vanmam* where the two Dalit communities Pallars and Parayrs were pitied against by the upper castes. Pallars considered themselves superior to Parayars. Sunderaju, a Pallar, declares: "The Parayars are inferior to us, and always will be. We are not untouchables, we are of royal descent. We are not Dalits. We are now Devendra Kula Vellalars or Mallars. So we must not have any type of contact or communication with those low Dalit Parayars (Bama, 2010, 77-78)." The question of existence and identity became a hurdle in his life to go ahead. Even his sister Nagi humiliated Limbale by calling him an outcaste: "You have no connection with us. Nobody knows where you come from. Our fathers are not the same (63)." Limbale was full of hatred for his mother in particular and the upper castes in general. His anger knew no bounds because of caste-discrimination and humiliation. He remarks: "Why didn't my mother abort me when I was a foetus? Why did she not strangle me as soon as I was born? We may be children born out of caste but that does not mean we must be humiliated. What exactly is our fault? Why should a child suffer for the sin of his parents? (64)" Sharankumar again opines: "...whenever I look at my mother I grow wild with anger. Why did she commit adultery at all? (64)" This shows the anger and pain of the children born out of illicit sex. This clearly shows that people love orthodox traditions rather than human beings.

Caste-discrimination became a problem for Limbale. When he was living at Ahmedpur, people of Lingayat community considered him Lingayat because of his name. Limbale dared not disclose his caste-identity. He was living in the house of an upper caste with his wife and sister Vani. He remarks: "If they come to know my caste they would drive me out of the house I had rented from a high caste landlord. I would be beaten badly. They would even torture my wife. My sister Vani now was living with me and I was afraid of losing my prestige (104)." When Limbale was transferred from Ahmedpur to Latur, he faced many problems to take a room on rent. People of Latur were caste-conscious. Caste had dehumanised all high caste people at Latur. The writer opines:

> I faced the problem of finding a house in a new town and my caste followed me like an enemy....was turned away wherever I went. They said frankly, 'we don't want to rent out our house to Muslims and Mahars'....I could not get a single room. Every town and person was caste conscious. This casteism had dehumanized everyone (106).

This is similar to Bama's difficulty in getting a room on rent. Bama wanted to take a small room on rent but wherever she went, the owners of the houses pestered her with hundreds of questions. She tells that they "questioned me about my village, my name, my parents, and my brothers and sisters. Endless questions about my job, my property, my jewels, and each one of my belongings (Bama, 2008, 120)." Women of the other castes didn't face this problem and could easily rent a house. She remarks: "I have to struggle so hard because I am a woman. And exactly like that, my people are punished constantly for the simple fact of having been born as Dalits (Bama, 2008, 120)."

The writer was always caught in a whirlwind. There was always the question of his identity. He belonged to a Mahar mother and a Patil father. He was brought up by his grandfather, Mahmood Dastagir Jamadar, a Muslim. He was always in a great dilemma. He thought that he shouldn't think himself as a high-caste, when his mother was an untouchable. His condition was like the devil Jarasandha of *Mahabharata*. One half of Limbale belonged to the village and other half was expelled. The writer observes: "I am like Jarasandh. Half of me belong to the village, whereas the other half is excommunicated. Who am I? To whom is my umbilical cord connected?" (38-39) Because of his caste, there arose a great problem in the marriage of Limbale. Whenever there was any marriage proposal for Limbale, his caste became a hurdle for him. Nobody was ready to marry his daughter to Limbale. Masamai's friend from Mang caste had a daughter and she was born from her illegitimate relations with a Patil. That girl was also a bastard like Limbale. So Limbale's mother and Kaka were planning to marry Limbale to that girl. He observes: "The girl I married needed to be a hybrid like me to ensure a proper match. A bastard must always be matched with another bastard. No one else will marry their daughters to a bastard like me (98)." This also shows the sub-human treatment and hypocrisy of Dalits. Limbale was judged by his caste not by his qualities. In the end, Limbale was married to Kusum. His in-laws refused to send Kusum with him. His mother-in-law said that there was, "no discipline in your house. You sell liquor there. All kinds of people visit you. Our daughter will be spoiled. You may take her when you start working. We won't send our daughter until you are independent (100)." Limbale visited his in-laws at Barshi to take his wife back. Limbale's father-in-law was always drunk and quarrelled with him when Limbale went there. His mother-in-law abused him and said: "You are rotten people. We have purified you. You were lying on the garbage (100)." This shows that people had crossed all limits of humanity. The ill-treatment of his in-laws shows that people are plagued by caste. Limbale was not liked by his father-in-law because of his relationship with his grandfather, a Muslim by religion. When Limbale visited his in-laws house, his father-in-law Maryappa Kamble argued with Limbale about the purity of blood of his family. Maryappa Kamble remarks:

> My son is a president of the Dalit Panthers. He is highly respected by his followers. You say that you are a relative of that Muslim. You are the cause of humiliation for us among our own caste. We had told everyone that you are of pure blood. You must have some self-respect, otherwise don't enter our house (101).

Limbale portrayed another example of caste-discrimination. Limbale was discriminated by the people of his own community because of his caste. Limbale's grandmother asked for Mallya's sister hand for Limbale. He was very happy to listen to this. But his happiness soon ceased. Because Mallaya's parents "refused the proposal because I was not of pure blood (92)."

Poverty and Hunger: Unbeaten Enemies

Poverty is the main reason of Dalits' exploitation and it is the same poverty that pushes them away from education. Due to poverty Dalit children had to leave school to support their families. Dalits didn't have much food to fill their belly. They were dependent on the leftover food of the high-castes. In this regard Mulk Raj Anand in his famous novel *The Untouchable* remarks: "They are helpless to collect the discarded food of the non-Dalits to satisfy their hunger (Anand, 1970, 25)." Limbale's friend Harya had to leave school to support his family. He was employed on Girmallaya's farm. For his hard work he received food and a hundred rupees a year. (1-2) At Dayanand College's hostel Dalits were forced to live with limited facilities. Limbale says:

> We continued our education amidst great poverty. We barely had money for a cup of tea. ...There were so many Dalit students like us. The pain of poverty was not just mine. We all existed like grains crushed in a stone grinder (83).

High-caste people were economically well-settled and powerful. Dalits were dependent on them for everything. To satisfy their hunger, Dalits sometimes did odd jobs. They started selling themselves. A woman "becomes a whore and a man a thief. The stomach makes you clean shit; it even makes you eat shit (8)." Limbale further remarks about hunger and poverty:

> Bhakari is as large as man. It is as vast as the sky, and bright like sun. Hunger is bigger than a man. Hunger is more vast than the seven circles of hell. Man is only as big as the bhakari, and only as big as his hunger. Hunger is more powerful than man. A single stomach is like the whole earth. Hunger seems no bigger than your open palm, but it can swallow the whole world and let out a belch. What about stealing and fighting? If there was no hunger what would have happened to sin and virtue, heaven and hell, this creation of God? If there was no hunger how could a country, its borders, citizens, parliament, Constitution come into being? The world is born from a stomach, so also the links between mother and father, sister and brother (50-51).

This is similar to what Girija Pryadershini has quoted Mahatma Gandhi who greatly influenced Anand's writings, describes

 The Famished Gods

about hunger: "Hunger knows no sin, even Drona and Bhishma, devadashis point to their bellies in justification of sin. Habit has dulled their sense of sin regarding their calling (Pryadershini, 2003, 183)." This is very similar to Laxman Gaikwad's observation, when he narrates his encounters with hunger and starvation. He said that he ate gruel made of cheap grain:

> We used to coarse-grind it. It was full of worms and insects but we were so hungry that we greedily drank that hot insect-ridden gruel without ever bothering to filter off the insects...When Bhau and Anna did not give me from their share, I used to lick my hands after rubbing them on the plate, and then lick the plate with my tongue. I used to stare at Bhau and Anna's gruel greedily. So even when they were hungry, they angrily offered me some of gruel from their shares, muttering, 'Lakshimanya is like a curse' (Gaikwad, 1998, 37-38).

Similarly Namdev Dhasal, a revolutionary poet, curses hunger in one of his poem titled "Hunger":

> Hunger, just tell us, to what race does this ape belong.
> If you can't answer that, we'll fuck seventeen generations of you.
> We'll fuck your mother, hunger... (Dhasal, 2010, 48)

During ox-festival, as it was customary, mostly odd jobs were assigned to Dalits. The chosen family member was assigned to do various jobs during the whole year like lighting the village street lamps, dragging the dead animal, skinning it and sold the skin. Dalits, "would give eight measures of jowar. Then everyone had a share in it and it helped to satisfy our hunger in a small way (13)."

After the quarrel between Masamai and grandmother Santamai, Santamai left Maharwada and she started living at the bus stand. Limbale left the Maharwada and came to live with Santamai at bus stand. Limbale said that from now onwards, "bus stand was like home. They "lay like discarded bus tickets (42)." They "waited at the bus stand for bus as a prostitute waits for her customers (41)." Dada took the job of the porter at the bus stand and carried the luggage of the villagers. Whatever he earned, he gave it to Santamai. Santamai swept the bus stand and the bus stand owner gave her a cup of tea in turn half of which she gave to Limbale. Though she swept the bus stand, she was not given respect as human being.

This is just as Bakha, the protagonist of Mulk Raj Annad's novel *The Untouchable* was treated inhumanly. Bakha says: "They think we are dirt because we clean their dirt (Anand, 1970, 68)." This reveals the miserable circumstances of Dalits who were treated as scums. Limbale experienced all the atrocities imposed on women when he lived with his grandmother Santamai at bus stand. Maharwada had no facilities when Limbale came to live with grandmother in the open area at bus stand. He says:

Initially we lived in the open behind the bus stand. We made stoves by arranging stones. Half the fire went waste because of the unruly wind. It was very difficult to make our bhakaris. My duty was to gather twigs, rags and bits of paper for fuel. If I picked up something from a farm its owner would beat me and drive me away. My hands and legs were bruised and torn by thorn pricks. We ate and lived in the open behind the bus stand. Four tin sheets offered us shelter during rainy season (42).

This is similar to Franz Fanon's description of blacks in America. He says:

The town belonging to the colonized people, or at least the native town, the Negro village, the medina, the reservation, is a place of ill fame, peopled by men of evil repute. They are born there, it matters little where or how; they die there; it matters not where, nor how. It is a world without spaciousness; men live there on the top of each other, and there huts are built one on the top of the other. The native town is a hungry town, starved to bread, of meat, of shoes, of coal, of light (Fanon, 2010, 30).

Untouchability: An Inerasable Disease

This shows a great resemblance between the misery of the untouchables and Africans. Untouchability was so rampant in society that even the school was not untouched by it. Limbale went to picnic with his teachers and students of upper castes of the school. The higher caste boys and girls were playing games at the picnic spot. Dalit students were not allowed to play games with the upper caste boys. Limbale observes:

The Wani and Brahmins boys played kabbadi. Being marked as Mahars we couldn't join them. So Mallaya, Umbrya, Parshya, all from my caste, began to play touch-and-go. We played one kind of game while the high-caste village boys played together. The two games played separately like two separate whirlwinds (2).

After playing the game, all the teachers and students sat under a tree to eat their food. The upper caste boys and girls "sat in a circle under a banyan tree. We, the Mahar boys and girls, were asked to sit under another tree (2)." The upper caste boys and girls opened their packets of food and offered their food to their teachers. The girls of the high castes, "offered us their curry and bhakaris without touching us (3)." This shows that even the school-going children of upper castes practise untouchability. Limbale's school was run in a temple of Ithoba. Dalit boys and girls were not allowed to sit inside the temple rather they were asked to sit at the entrance of the temple. When Limbale went to attend the school at Shivappa Teli's mansion and sat with other boys. Sharankumar said that the servant Mahadya came, "Running up to me he snatched my school bag and slapped me (5)." This is similar to what Raj Kumar has quoted Freeman in *Bheda*:

> The villagers never forget, nor did they let us forget that we were untouchables. High caste children sat inside the school; the Bauri children about twenty of us, sat outside on the veranda and listened. The two teachers, a Brahmin outsider, and temple servant refused to touch us, even with a stick. To beat us, they threw bamboo canes. The higher caste children threw mud at us. Fearing severe beatings we dared not fight back (Kumar, 2017, xx).

When during rainy season the school was held in the Marwari mansion, "Mahar boys had to sit on the floor whereas the other boys sat on a raised platform (5)."

Dalits were called Hindus by faith but they were exploited and subjugated by the so-called Hindus. Regarding this K. M. Panikkar observes: "...the Dalits were the submerged base of Hindu society, but the self assertion of the upper caste and the spiritual aspect enabled them to preserve their autonomy over the Dalits (Panikkar, 1961, 21)." Dalits were not allowed to visit Hindu temples and were "branded as untouchables.... High-caste children from the village may visit temple, yet we are forbidden (4-5)."

Dalits were not only discriminated in the matter of caste and religion, they were also discriminated and exploited in the matter of water at the bank of the river. There was varna-system on the banks of the river. The upper part of the river water was meant for Brahmins, Kshtriyas, Vaishyas and Shudras. The lowest part was meant for the untouchables:

> The high-caste villagers filled their water pots and their women washed their clothes upstream. Downstream the kunbies and shepherds collected water in their vessels and carried them off. They also washed their clothes and bathed. Those who looked after the grazing cattle washed their buffaloes and bathed themselves. The water at the lowest end was meant for us (7).

Dalits were not allowed to drink water from the well of the high-castes because they were considered impure and untouchables. Regarding to this Romila Thapar quoted a Chinese Buddhist Monk Fah Hian to point out how even the touch or the shadow of an Untouchable was thought to be polluting by the upper classes: "...the untouchables had to sound a clapper in the streets of the town so that people were warned of their presence; and that if an untouchable came into close range, the upper caste person would have to perform a ritual ablution (Thapar, 2002, 9)." In this context, Alok Mukherjee in his Introduction to the translation of Sharankumar Limbale's book titled *Towards an Aesthetic of Dalit Literature: History, Controversies and Considerations* has observed:

> The work of the Dalits is essential for maintaining the upper caste Hindus' purity. If they did not clean latrines, skin dead animals, and remove the carcasses, the social life of the upper caste will be unclean, polluted and diseased. And yet, just as these are revolting activities, so is the Dalit an object of revulsion, precisely for doing them, even though it is the upper caste Hindu who forces Dalits into carrying them out. Dalits enable the purity of upper caste society and become impure in the process (Mukherjee, 2004, 3).

Limbale has portrayed another incident of untouchability. When he was a small boy he played the game of vulture and dead animals with his playmates. There was a, "Mang boy who was a 'vulture', but who even as we played, kept his distance as he was not supposed to mix with us (15)." This clearly shows that Dalits were not discriminated by the upper castes but even by lower castes like Mang. The Mangs didn't want to touch the Mahars. Mahars were the Dalits of the Dalits. There is caste-discrimination even within Dalits. Once during summer season Limbale was playing with his friend Arjya, a boy of Mang community. They both were very thirsty. Limbale brought the Mang boy to his house for water. Santamai shouted angrily: "Why do you play with that boy? Is there no one else in the whole village to play with? Don't give him water in that vessel. If he touches it, he'll defile it (20). Mahar and Mang had their own separate banks at the river. They were not allowed to drink water from, "Different parts of the river bank were reserved for Mahars and Mangs (20)." Similarly, Parshya asks Shobhi:

> So you call us Mahars, don't you? Your water gets impure if we touch it, if that's so then why doesn't this river turn impure? If a human being becomes impure by our mere touch then why didn't your colour change to green or yellow, as it happens when someone is sick or poisoned? Why didn't the food in your bundle rot? (71).

Limbale has given many examples of the practice of untouchability. When during vacations Limbale came home, he with his friend visited the tea-shop of Shivram. At shop, "separate cup and saucer were kept for the Mahars and Mangs (76)." The upper-caste shopkeepers didn't receive any money directly from the hands of the Mahars and Mangs. Mahars and Mangs, "put the money for the tea on the ground or drop it from a height into the hands of the owner because for a Mahar or Mang to hand money directly to anyone was a sin (76)."

Dalit women were exploited in the name of caste, class and religion everywhere. Regarding the status of women in society, Simone de Beauvoir, in *The Second Sex*, says:

> Thus humanity is male and man defines woman not in herself but as relative to him: she is not regarded as an autonomous being. . . . For him she is sex — absolute sex, no less. She is defined and differentiated with reference to man and not he with reference to her; she is the incidental, the inessential as opposed to the essential. He is the Subject, he is the Absolute — she is the Other (Beauvoir, 1988, 16).

The Famished Gods

They were considered very low and degraded in life. Their miseries knew no end. Due to poverty and hunger, Santamai started the business of selling liquor and faced many difficulties in running such a business. Sometimes a drunkard tried to seduce her. Maharwada's neighbouring street was full of drunkards. The drunkards took the liquor from the house of Mahar but they refused to take water from them. They "had affairs with Mahar women but wouldn't accept the food they cooked (35)." Regarding this, Gail Omvedt says: "Men are at the top and women of that caste are on the bottom like crushed and wasted powder. And the very bottom is the Dalits and below them are the suppressed Dalit women (Omvedt, 321)." In this context Limbale in his novel *Hindu* has documented how a Dalit woman was disrobed by the upper caste people: "Draupadi, the character in *Mahabharata*, was not stripped naked. But Draupadi in independent India...was stripped naked..., because she was a dalit. The crowd encircled the naked Draupadi.... She stood there naked, spears struck to her body. A horrible silence fell all over the scene (Limbale, 2010, 146)."

The writer's father Ithal Kamble worked as a bonded labourer in the house of Hanmanta Limbale and was paid seven or eight hundred rupees for a year. He was no less than an animal who worked day and night. Hanmanta Limbale was very shrewd who ruined the family of Masamai and Ithal Kamble. Masamai divorced Ithal Kamble under the pressure of caste council. After divorce she was utterly lonely and helpless. Ithal Kamble took with him his two sons and he remarried a widow. But in our society, a woman was not allowed to remarry. A male could remarry and keep a concubine. As Kathamuthu a Dalit leader in *The Grip of Change* had a wife and a concubine. Limbale remarks: "A man can eat paan and spit as many times as he likes, but the same is not possible for a woman. It is considered wrong if a woman does that. Once her chastity is lost it can never be restored (36)." Regarding this, Monika Gupta writes about Dalit women: "...they have succumbed to brutalities by castiest groups and have undergone traumas at different level (Gupta, 2011, 101)." This shows that in our patriarchal society women are treated like commodities. A man can take his own decision but a woman is prohibited to do so.

The Famished Gods

When Masamai was alone and had no shelter, Hanmanta Limbale, "lured Masamai. She was given a rented house at Akkalkot (36)." She became, "pregnant, and gave birth to a son (36)." Limbale compared himself to Karna and his mother to Kunti. He says: "My first birth must have threatened the morality of the world. With my first cry at birth, milk must have splashed from the breasts of Kunti (36)."

Many questions were aimed at directly at upper caste Hindu society and its hypocrisy. These questions contained a lot of anger, agony, displeasure, resistance and protest in them. In *The Outcaste*, Limbale presents a string of such questions:

> Why did my mother say yes to the rape which brought me into this world? Why did she put up with the fruit of this illegitimate intercourse for nine months and nine days and allow me to grow in the foetus? Why did she allow this bitter embryo to grow? How many eyes must have humiliated her because they considered her a whore? Did anyone distribute sweets to celebrate my birth? Did anyone admire me affectionately? Did anyone celebrate my naming ceremony? Which family would claim me as its descendant? Whose son am I, really? (37)

These questions show Limbale's anguish and pain and also question of identity. He is neither a Dalit nor a Patil. Upper caste Patils, "in every village have made whore of the wives of Dalit farm labourers (38)." Even the small girls were not safe. As soon as a, "poor Dalit girl on attaining puberty has invariably been a victim of their lust. There is a whole breed to adulterous Patils (38)." For their survival in the village, the women of the, "Dalit families that survive by pleasuring the Patils sexually (38)" were bound to surrender to what they never desired willingly.

Dalit women submitted meekly to the lust of upper-castes merely for their livelihood and survival. The writer remarks: "Our villagers have provided us with bread so we owe much to them. They did provide bread but in exchange satisfied their lust with our women. I can't bear to think Masamai caught between bread and lust (64)." Upper caste fellows could rape Dalit women, as they desired but Dalits were not even allowed to see the women of upper castes sheepishly. To see an upper caste woman in a lustful manner was a serious crime. Once a boy of Dalit community committed that crime, the upper castes attacked the whole Maharwada. Besides this many Dalit men were put in jail. Their wives, "had been raped when their husbands were in prison. A village always acts atrociously like this against Dalits (71)." Whenever an animal died in the village, Dalits were considered responsible for it. Upper caste men "tied us to a pole and beat us like animals. They accused us of having poisoned the animal. Our women and children cried and shrieked. All the men in the Maharwada were very badly beaten (78)."

When the people of Maharwada were ostracized, Dalits said that the upper caste farmers "didn't allow us to come near the boundaries of their fields (79)." When Dalit women approached the boundaries of the upper castes' fields to graze their cattle, the farmers drove them away. The whole Dalit community was branded as monstrous. Even Dalit women, "were beaten as if they were slaves. Some farmers even harassed them sexually, pulled them into the crop, and raped them (79)."

Superstitions: A Brahminical Way of Exploitation

Dalits and all other backward castes were subjected to the shackles of superstitions. The backwards castes offered their first born to God. In the same way, Mahars also offered their first born to God and Goddesses like Ambabai, Yallama, Laxmi, Khandona, Masoba Satwai. If, "it is a son he is named Ambadas....and a girl is called Murali (92-93)." Devadasi system was the most prominent among Dalits. It was not God made but man-made. A girl, "who dedicated to God is never married because she is supposed to have already married to God (93)." Such a girl was exploited by the upper castes in various ways. It was very clear that a religious colour was given to the ritual prostitution. Limbale observes: "Such a girl called devadasi can live with a man she loves after performing certain rituals. The children born to devadasis are considered impure by blood and are not entitled to trade or work in a village. They live by begging (93)." This is similar to what William Dalrymple observes:

The devadasis stand in the direct line of one of the oldest institutions in India....Today, the devdasis are drawn exclusively from the lowest castes—usually from the Dalit Madar caste—and are almost entirely illiterate. The majority of modern devdasis in Karnataka are

The Famished Gods

straightforward sex workers... They usually work from home rather than in brothels or on the streets, and tend to start younger than commercial sex workers. Nevertheless, the main outlines of their working lives are in reality little different from those of others in the sex-trade (Dalrymple, 2018, n.p.).

This is very clear that Dalits were exploited in the name of God. It was believed that if the devdasi-families refused to dedicate their girl children to the goddess, the curse would fall upon them. Amita Trasi in her novel *The Colour of Our Sky* has also observed that Mukta's grandmother told her daughter when she refused to dedicate Mukta to devadasi tradition: "You will anger the deity. We will have to live with her curse if you insult our tradition. It was decided for us the day we were born. What tradition? What was decided? That we are going to sleep with men in the name of God, that we are servants of God but the wife of the entire village? (Trasi, 2017, 21)" Women were the most sufferers. The upper castes used them for satisfying their lust. The children born of such Dalit women were considered outcaste and denied their due place in society. They were denied self dignity and honour. They were dehumanised by this so-called Hindu society that is based on the principle of spiritual equality.

This incident of humiliation deeply penetrated Limbale's heart to the core. He stated his helplessness, pain and insult due to hollow customs and traditions. He remarks: "I was ashamed of the culture. I was terribly angry at its customs, but I was helpless. I had suffered the pain of insults. The thought of marriage was intolerable to me. The thought of selecting a girl as a match shocked me like acid thrown on me. I didn't want such shocks. It was better to stay unmarried (92)."

Education: A Tool of Resistance

Higher education has instilled in Dalits a new wave of revolution. It made Limbale more conscious about exploitation, humiliation and discrimination that Dalits were experiencing for centuries. Limbale remarks:

While studying in college I was mentally aflame. I was growing amidst a conflagration. The roots of the Movement were setting more firmly. Injustice towards us was assuming a new meaning. We were awakening under a new consciousness which was becoming more pervasive day by day (83).

This is similar to what Bama has observed in an interview. She says:

We have been resisting from the beginning. Now because Dalits are politically more aware, educationally a little better off, these become threatening to the oppressors. Dalits want change; whether it is in religion, politics or in literature, but their oppressors don't want it. When they want to celebrate their freedom and assert themselves, upper castes want to oppress them again. That is what Bhima Kaoregaon is about. Una showed that a cow is more important than a Dalit life. It shows that they are treated less than animals (Dutta, 2018, 6).

Limbale was greatly influenced by Dr. B. R. Ambedkar. He greeted his friends by saying 'Jai Bhim' instead of 'Namaskar'. He remarks:

I stopped saying 'namaskar' and started saying 'Jai Bhim' instead. I substituted Babasaheb for Ambedkar since it sounded less formal and more respectful. My youth had assumed a new meaning and significance. The blood flowed like hot lava through my body. My mind burned with myriad thoughts in silent protest. Babasaheb filled me with reverence. I felt I was meeting my mother of the last seven births. I burned within myself whenever I heard the news about the atrocities against Dalits (86-87).

Dalits were denied their right to education for centuries. They were ill-treated like dumb cattle. Reservation is a powerful tool for Dalits to enter in educational institutions where they were not supposed to enter. Without reservation, they were helpless and all their paths of success would be blocked. When Limbale was in college, he came to know that reservation facilities of Dalits would be cancelled. He became restless and was scared. He remarks:

If these facilities are cancelled, give us our own Dalisthan. We are educated only because these facilities exist; they were like a father to us. If there were no facilities we would have had no such education, would have been at home grazing cattle and helping our parents. Instead we were living in cities away from home, in order to get an education. Our parents were toiling to death there, I often thought of their hard labour, hunger, and hopes for our future. On every page whatever book I read, I saw pictures of Santamai begging and Dada's hard work as a porter. Whenever we heard news that our mothers and sisters in the village were tortured we couldn't concentrate on our studies because we were so angry and frustrated (89).

This shows the anger of the writer against the rotten and exploitative system of society. Regarding this, Sudha Pai has pointed out:

Assertion in this context means to question or challenge the unequal hierarchical caste structure and the resisting of norms of purity and pollution provided in the Manusmriti - that have placed the Dalit or ex-untouchable at the bottom, below the line of pollution. Dalit assertion therefore is a strident revolt or upsurge from below by the Dalits against being social outcastes. Such a revolt has a distinct meaning for our democracy - it means going beyond normal forms of democratic participation - to movements and actions aimed at breaking down structures of inequality leading to social transformation (Pai, 2013, xvii-xviii).

There were riots between Hindus and Dalits at Ahmedpur. The reason behind these riots was that Hindus didn't tolerate that Dalits would get education and do jobs. Dalits were demanding the renaming of Marathwada University to Dr. B. R. Ambedkar. The houses of the Dalits were set ablaze during day time. The writer remarks:

The Hindu community was hurt, because with the facilities given to them, Dalits were getting education and becoming aware of their rights. A generation of militant youths generated by the movement also threatened the Hindus and the thought of untouchables living contented lives with jobs made available to them, irritated them. Dalits refused to do the lowly jobs that they once did for Hindus. Such changes in the Dalit community occurred with their conversion to Buddhism. The thought that the community which had lived the life of cats and dogs for thousands of years was now behaving as equals was unacceptable to the high caste Hindus (103).

There was a meeting once held in the context of celebration of Dr. B.R. Ambedkar's birth anniversary. Limbale was also invited in the meeting. But he didn't go to attend it because there were arguments between Limbale and a man of the organisation the day before celebration. The leader remarks: "Limbale sahib we are of pure blood. Those people living down there are impure. ...Don't be on their side at the meeting tomorrow? (106)" Limbale expressed that the President didn't know the reality of his birth. Limbale and his wife Kusum decided to take part in the birth anniversary of Dr. B.R. Ambedkar. Limbale writes: "...What would happen if the volunteers of this vast Dalit movement came to know that I was impure? Would they too avoid and ostracize me? (106)"

Conclusion

To conclude, it can be said that hunger and poverty run throughout the lives of Dalits. This leads to the exploitation of Dalits at all levels. This hunger is external as well as internal. Dalits are subjugated by the upper castes and sometimes they had to submit themselves for their survival and livelihood. Through his autobiography, Sharankumar Limbale makes the world aware of the plight of Dalits and being an outcaste. He was an outsider in his own house. He was doubly exploited—being Dalit and being an outcaste. His saga of pain is a symbol of his struggle, his quest for identity and existence. He has brought out the dark side of his family and upper caste to the forefront. Writers like Bama, Baby Kamble, Daya Pawar, Laxman Mane, Laxman Gaikwad have depicted the exploitation and discrimination of Dalits. Limbale's autobiography *The Outcaste: Akkarmashi* is a unique autobiography that documents the exploitation and subjugation of Dalits as well as the pain of an outcaste.

❏

Chapter-5

The Contested Identities

- Bidisha Pal

Introduction

The literary movement of the Dalits started following the Dalit Panther movement of 1972. Maharashtra, known to be the seedbed of the movement witnesses the assertion of Dalit writers, critics, and poets to launch fiery battles against the existing hegemony of the society with the power of writing. Dalit literature is the literary outburst of the age-old injustice and pent-up emotions and anger of the Dalits. Basisth (2016) has detailed the nature of the genre as "Writers share their own experiences of social and communal iniquity. Their writings were the outburst of their suppressed feelings, which has come down from generations. The Educated Dalits are spreading awareness and making oppressed acquaint with their rights through their intellectual discourse (21)." According to Limbale (2004), Dalit literature works on an alternative aesthetic which depends on, "first, the artist's social commitment; second, the life-affirming values present in the artistic creation; and third, the ability to raise the reader's consciousness of fundamental values like equality, freedom, justice and fraternity (120)."

Dalit autobiography or life writing is the primary genre of literary expression for the Dalit writers. The genre deals with the socio-political history and trauma of casteist politics and ekes out the "lived experience" of the Dalit community. In Maharashtra, the first Dalit autobiography was written by Daya Pawar entitled as *Baluta* (1978) which was later translated by Jerry Pinto. *Majya Jalmachi Chittarkatha* (1983) by Shantabai Krishnaji Kamble was the first Dalit autobiography by a woman. A number of Dalit autobiographies like *Jeena Amucha* or *The Prisons we Broke* by Baby Kamble (translated by Maya Pandit, 2008), *Aayadan* or *The Weave of My Life: A Dalit Woman's Memoirs* by Urmila Pawar (translated by Maya Pandit, 2009) and *Uchyala* or *The Branded* by Laxman Gaikwad (translated by P.L. Kolharkar, 1988) have championed the cause of the literary mobilization of the Dalits.

An autobiography often tends to be a bildungsroman dealing with the discourse of moral, psychological, and spiritual discourse of an individual. The bildungsroman, in the process, constructs identities for individuals. A man has to live with twofold identities. One is the personal identity that owes its existence to the individual self and self-investigation; it is the intrapersonal bond between one's self and personality. Another is the social identity that manifests the communicational and interpersonal relationship between a man and his society to which he belongs. It is said that men are the socialized organism. Through narrating his own life a man redefines and reappraises the identity formation process. In case of Dalit autobiographies, which are again biographies of the narrators' communities besides his own self, the social identity becomes a *raison d' etre* for existence and a process of imbibing the social traits. The study focuses on *Akkarmashi* or *The Outcaste*, the autobiography of Sharankumar Limbale that was originally written in Marathi and translated into English by Santosh Bhoomkar in 2003. The narrative is a budding bildungsroman and portrays the journey of Limbale's life amidst a number of struggles and odds towards the realization of being a half-caste or an *akkarmashi* being born of a father who is a high caste Patil and a mother who is a lower caste Mahar woman. Limbale (2003) says, "I am an Akkarmashi (half-caste). I am condemned, branded illegitimate (ix)." Throughout the narrative, the narrator produces instances of difficulties and existential crisis of being a half-caste or an outcaste of the society. Social identity enables a man to designate his position in society and strengthen the relationship with the other members of the society that surround him. Being deprived of the social identity Limbale suffers from an identity crisis that becomes a prime mover in his quest for self. Each and every character Limbale encounters in his life entangles and makes his position crucial again and again. That he belongs to neither the upper caste nor the lower caste makes both his self and existence a Dalit among the Dalits.

Through a detailed analysis of the text and study of the socio-political and historical background of the Dalits with theoretical methodology, the article extends its investigation to the aspects of identity and existential crisis in *The Outcaste* and shows how the contested identities of Limbale's life produce contested moments of struggle for sustenance and social epiphanies.

Being a Dalit: The Crisis of Existence

'Dalit'- the very word comes from the Sanskrit *Dalita* or *Dalan* which means crushed, made to the ground, or broken to pieces. The word was first coined by Jotirao Phule in the nineteenth century in the context of the oppression faced by the 'untouchable' castes or those who belonged to the lowest of the low rank of the hierarchical ladder of Hindu casteist society. They were designated as the "depressed classes" by the British in the colonial period and possessed thereafter different names like *Harijan, Chandala, Asprushya, Atishudra*, etc.

Though stipulated for a particular sect, the connotation of 'Dalit' has become many in terms of different parameters and dimensions. A Dalit can be anyone who is oppressed by race, class, caste, gender, economy, history, and politics. Kandasamy has shown in her article (2008) "To a man, a woman is the Dalit of the house" (para 4). Limbale says in an interview (2004), "We need a language that speaks to all the dispossessed, wherever they may be, whichever country, whichever community. Whether they are savarna or non-White, if they are downtrodden and exploited, they are one of us (137)." The oppression and torments aid in constructing the distinct voice and identity of the Dalit. The literary expressions also embrace the distinctness. A Dalit autobiography is the life and identity of a Dalit within a particular community. In another interview, Limbale speaks about his autobiography, "Truly speaking, it is the autobiography of the entire Dalit community. Whatever experience I have shared in the book, I have written on behalf of my community. The very essence of Dalit literature is community feeling. We talk in chorus as representatives of a community. The word 'I' is insignificant in Dalit literature. It is 'we' that matters. Thus Akarmashi is not only my story; it is the story of every Dalit (3)."

The Maharwada in his autobiography is a microcosm for the divergent representations of the Mahars, the Mangs, the Patils, the Brahmins, and the Muslims who intersect each other in their struggles for establishment and acceptability in the society. Limbale weaves a world of the Dalit community through the depictions of various characters who suffer from an existential crisis. The prime mover and agential factor of this world is caste and casteist afflictions, it is the caste-ridden world where his mother Masamai, his grandmother Santamai, all his sisters and brothers Nagi, Nirmi, Vani, Sooni, Pami, Tamma or Shrikant, Indira , and Sridamma, his grandfather dada, the community people, his friends and the woman he loves from the deep core of his heart are all entangled in the strange web of 'dalitized' existence, the feeling of being in a world that constantly takes a toll of their lives and dreams to make even both ends meet. To him, "This is the story of my life, an expression of my mother's agony and an autobiography of a community (Limbale, 2003, xxiii)." It is a world where hunger, poverty, and day to day struggle for bare and minimum sustenance are everyday realities. During the troubled narrative journey, many events are interspersed throughout which point fingers to the 'dalitized' self of Limbale's community. It is the very essence of the dalitized being that makes his mother a victim to the clutches of the lust of the upper caste male members of the society. Limbale says in the acknowledgments about his mother, "It is through the Dalit movement and Dalit literature that I understood that my mother was not an adulteress but the victim of a social system (ix)." One can remember the helpless condition of women who face sexual exploitations in Daya Pawar's *Baluta* (1978) and also in *Golpitha* (1973) by Namdeo Dhasal where he depicts the red light area consisting of Dalit women.

Limbale starts with an account of a school picnic where the Mahar students and the Wani and Brahmin students both take part. The torments of being in the downtrodden sections of society start to take a shape from the period of childhood. Limbale shows the method of smooth seclusion of the Mahar students from the beginning: "Play over, we settled down to eat. Boys and girls from the high castes like Wani, Brahmin, Marwari, Muslim, Maratha, Teli, fishermen, goldsmiths, and all the teachers, about hundred or so sat in a circle under a banyan tree. We, the Mahar boys and girls, were asked to sit under another tree (Limbale, 2003, 2)." Thus, educational institutes like schools which seem an anti-caste space and vouch for equality and universality of recognition for all the students emerge out to be a caste-ridden physical space. The essence of being a Dalit reflects in the behavior of the upper caste students too: "The high-caste girls from our village offered us their curry and bhakaris without touching us. The thought that they might have seen our food upset me. I was ashamed of my food and felt guilty eating it (Limbale, 2003, 3)." In *Joothan-An Untouchable's Life* (2003) by Valmiki, the school is depicted as the casteist place where the upper caste headmaster Kaliram humiliates the students of the *chuhra* community by making them sweeping the ground of the school premises in front of all the *tyaga* teachers. Valmiki very sadly remembers the insulting remarks of the teachers: "The taunts of my teachers and fellow students pierced me deeply. 'Look at this *chuhre ka,* pretending to be a Brahmin' (71)." The practice of untouchability is prevalent even among the Christian missionary convents as pointed out by Bama in *Karukku* (1992). Devy in his introduction (2003) of *The Outcaste* says that: "Even Islam and Christianity did not escape the fate of being fragmented in caste terms when they were received in India (xv)." Similarly, in his autobiography *Surviving in My World* (2015) Manohar Mouli Biswas, the Bengali Dalit poet has depicted the ill-treatment of the teachers in school that makes his *jetha* so angry that he is provoked to a give a sound beating to the teacher.

Another incident of insult and shame occurs to Limbale during the wedding ceremony of the surrounding villages where the Maharwada people have to wait outside the wedding house to have the leftover food of the feast. On one such occasion, Limbale and his family are given plateful of *kheer* or sweet delicacies. When he sneaks some of the *kheer* in a plate for his mother in the house, he is positively thrashed and reprimanded from the upper caste Girimallya: "They scum! They eat as much as they want and still crave for more to take home (Limbale, 2003, 9)." Limbale has another realization of existential crisis when he portrays his playing with a Mang boy Arjya which causes many grievances to Santamai: "Are you born from the seed of a Mang that you keep their company? You are the son of the village head. You must eat and play like a prince. You are the son of a Patil...'Santamai went on shouting at me (Limbale, 2003, 20)." That he is not only a Dalit and somebody stands in a much lower position makes Limbale conscious of the pricking torments of a caste-ridden world.

As the narrative progresses and Limbale marches towards maturity and adulthood, the Dalitized experience gets concretized. He bears witness to the poor Dalit girls who have been given to the high caste Patils' lusts by the Dalit families because pleasing them sexually would make them survive. He recalls the atrocities on the Dalit men perpetrated by the upper caste men who torment the Dalit men in the prison and rape the Dalit women. He describes Shobhi who is a representative of the upper caste before him and Parshya only to remind them of their lower-caste status: "Shobhi stood before us as a symbol of the caste system. Her feet, her thighs, her arms, her face-everything was a part of the system she belonged to (Limbale, 2003, 71)." However, after attaining youth he gets involved in the Ambedkarite philosophy and shed the cringing and paralyzing Dalitized existence to a revolting and evolutionary one. In college too he recalls the hostel atmosphere: "All the boys in our hostel were Dalit. It was more or less like a camp. We were awed by our great struggle. I stopped saying 'namaskar' and started saying 'Jai Bhim' instead (Limbale, 2003, 86)." The renaming of Marathwada University as Dr. Babasaheb Ambedkar University and the Dalit Panther Movements towards the liberation of the Dalits get prominent in due course. There is a lot of struggle, protest, police *lathi* charges, and activism involved in the movements. Limbale witnesses the Dalits' progress towards newer emancipation, "The procession of restless Dalit youths was moving. The riots and agitation due to the renaming of the university had not been died down yet (Limbale, 2003, 106)."

Such minute references from the narrative condition the mode of the narrative. It points out the very fact of being a Dalit and having the Dalitized selves. The 'physical apartheid' that the Dalits are subject to constitute the very Dalitized selves and sentiments when they are segregated out of the mainstream society and face humiliation. The experience of passing through the purity-pollution policy is shared and common to every Dalit.

Fractured Identity: "Who am I"?

According to The Social Identity theory of the social psychologists Tajfel and Turner (1979, 1986), a person's self is determined by the social group he belongs to. A person cannot only live upon his personal selfhood; he has to carry multiple selves, roles, and identities that the group assigns him to. Inhabiting in a particular group determines a person's actions, behaviors, activities, and attitude towards the other group members he shares an association with. A person might act differently according to relative social contexts. Tajfel and Turner further subdivide the social groups into ingroup and outgroup and mention three processes that aid in creating the ingroup/outgroup mentality. One is Social Categorization in which people's identities are categorized in terms of color, caste, class, creed, religion, etc. Another is Social Identification in which the people of a particular group category adopt the identity and behave to be a particular member of that group. The third is Social Comparison in which the members of a particular group tend to compare their categories with the members of another particular group. The more comparisons are made, the more the members of an ingroup get intimated with each other. This, in one way, provides strength and confidence among the residing members and in another constructs the binary of 'us' and 'them' as well.

The social identity turns to be a fractured reality for Limbale. He neither feels to be attached to any of the processes of ingroup/ outgroup social categorization. The identity that is thrust upon him is a confused paranoia that makes him dwindling over a tumultuous life. Limbale speaks out in disgust:

> My father and forefathers were Lingayat. Therefore I am one too. My mother was Mahar. My mother's father and forefathers were Mahar; hence I am also a Mahar. From the day I was born until today, I was brought by my grandfather Mahmood Dastagir Jamadar. My grandfather in the sense he lives with my grandmother, Santamai. Does this mean I am Muslim as well? Then why can't the Jamadar's affection claim me as Muslim? How can I be high caste when my mother is untouchable? If I am untouchable, what about my father who is a high caste? I am like Jarasandh. Half of me belongs to the village, whereas the other half is excommunicated. Who am I? To whom is my umbilical cord connected? (Limbale, 2003, 38-39)

Limbale falls into a crisis of situation because of his fractured identity for a number of times in his life. The person he fondly calls Kaka is known to be the father of his sisters and brother while his own father Hanmanta Patil sheds off the responsibility of his son making Limbale an unacceptable lot in the society. His fate is like that of Karna of the epic *The Mahabharata*, who was an illegitimate reproduction of Kunthi and the Sun God and was readily immersed into the river by his mother after birth. Throughout his life, Karna had to bear the name Sutaputra in spite of having the royal blood and lineage within him. Similarly, Limbale has been the ill-fated son of his Mahar mother Masamai who is unable to provide him the upper caste lineage that he is biologically entitled to for coming off the Lingayat father. This is sadly reflected in Limbale: "After my birth the mansions of the Patil community must have become tense. My first breath must have threatened the morality of the world. With my first cry at birth, milk must have splashed from the breasts of every Kunti (Limbale, 2003, 36)."

Limbale recalls one incident in school when his name has to be registered according to the bearing of his father's entitlement of a Patil but when his father happens to know the fact, he proceeds with three or four rowdies to call the matter off. Such disgust he carries within his mind about his own son. Even the person kaka also gives no respite to the hapless souls of Limbale and his family. Though he frequents the family often, his own house is barred for Limbale. "Once I spotted Kaka in a mansion. That's how, at last, I discovered Kaka's mansion. Expecting to be noticed and invited in, I deliberately lingered by Kaka's mansion, but the moment he noticed me he shut the door. I returned home with a sad face (Limbale, 2003, 46)."

The sense of utter dejection from every sphere of society becomes a haunting metaphor throughout Limbale's life. It is because of his illegitimate identity, his "impure blood" that he loses the first love of his life Shewantha whom he cannot marry. On another occasion his marriage proposal is nearly called off when the bride's family comes to know of his illegitimacy: "Mallya's parents had refused the proposal because I was not of pure blood. These people love conventions more than they do human beings (Limbale, 2003, 92)." Social identity determines one's personality among the other members of the society, but when someone deviates from it, it creates corruptible change in the attitude of the members. Hence, instead of the 'us' and 'them' binary of social groups, it becomes a 'them' and 'me' for Limbale because he belongs to nowhere of the social identities. He is the *Mestizo* born of the mixed caste Indian parentage that is deprived mentally and physically of every sort of social right. Even after marriage, he does not get proper respect from his in-laws. His identity causes him nothing but occasional abuses, fisticuffs, and insults. His mother-in-law keeps saying to him, "You are rotten people. We have purified you. You were lying on the garbage' (Limbale, 2003, 100)." His multiple identities of being Mahar, Lingayat, and Muslim produce contested moments of uneasiness and harassments. Limbale reflects sadly, "So a Muslim can't be my relative because his religion is different from mine. We are like animals of different species. Such discrimination between one offspring and the other (Limbale, 2003, 101)" has become our destiny.

Throughout the journey of life, Limbale makes a quest to get the answer to "Who *am* I?" The doubly tormented life consisting of both casteist afflictions and an outcaste position complicates the journey to be the troubled metaphor of life. The crisis of situation further congeals into crucial ties when Limbale cannot be a part of the procession of Ambedkar's birth anniversary celebration, "People in the procession were all pure Mahars, but what about me with my impure blood? I felt extremely sad about my low birth. So what about me? I am a whirlwind (Limbale, 2003, 106)."

His troublesome identity provokes him to make a social transformation lest his caste is revealed among others. The modern social mobilization among the Dalits to shed the Dalitness from their lives and accept the Hindu norms can be seen in the narrative when Limbale hides his caste by saluting "Namaskar" instead of "Jay Bhim" so that he appears to be an upper caste Lingayat. "If I happened to be going with a high-caste friend and someone greeted me with a 'Jay Bhim' I felt like an outsider (Limbale, 2003, 104)." He even avoids acquaintance with his Santamai and dada when they visit him. The tendency to conceal the Dalit identity is a reactionary attitude on part of the Dalits. Heering (2017) points out in an article, "In reaction to the discrimination and the change of behavior that results when their identity is uncovered, many Dalits recount-some with embarrassment-their attempts to conceal their Dalitness (214)." It is also notable to some extent in Mallya, Limbale's old friend whom he meets in Sholapur. Owing to the social identity transformation Mallya is seen to shed the Dalit identity to become a "sahib" now: "Though born a Dalit he had not read Dalit literature (Limbale, 2003, 112)" and this reflects in the manner of living he and his family undertakes:

> Mallya's mother was rather uncomfortable while she talked to me. Once upon a time this woman, Hiramashi, used to wear rags, as she had no cloths, and had gone around gathering dung. This woman who used to wear a nine-yard sari was now in a six-yard sari like a modern woman. Instead of a bodice she wore a blouse. She had also changed her hair style. Mallya, her son, was now a sahib, hence this transformation. The mother of sahib should live accordingly (Limbale, 2003, 112).

The process of the immolation of identity equates with the notion of 'mimicry' propounded by Bhabha (1994) which is a technique of "camouflage…against a mottled background, of becoming mottled (para 1)." The mimicry gives birth to an ambivalent, hybridized, and marginalized colonial subject "that is almost the same but not quite (Bhabha, 1994, para 5)." But the process of mimicry has the continuous production of "its excess, its slippage, its difference (Bhabha, 1994, para 5)." Hence, Limbale's act of miming the role of an upper caste makes prominent the fractured identity once again. He is an outsider to the Dalits and to the upper castes as well. Thus, he is thrown into an ambivalent position. This leads to an existential crisis: "I was a Dalit who had become a Brahmin by attitude, but high-caste people didn't even allow me to stand at their doorsteps. Either I should live in Bhimnagar, or in the Dalit locality or even in a Muslim locality. I was an outcaste in all other localities (Limbale, 2003, 107)."

From a Casteist World to an Outcaste World

I was afraid of my caste because I couldn't claim my father's caste and religion. In a sense, I was not a Mahar, because high-caste blood ran in my body. Could I drain this blood out of my body? My own body nauseated me (Limbale, 2003, 82).

One's caste is determined by his origin from which one descends. The five-fold caste system that was described in *Manusmriti* subjects the untouchables to the lowermost sanctum of the hierarchical ladder. The *Jal-Achal* or the untouchable Dalits construct their

The Famished Gods

fates according to the rules of the upper caste. The Dalits are the community people. In every Dalit autobiography, the depiction of a casteist world becomes the *tour de force* for pushing the narrative forward. However, although *Akkarmashi* tends to portray the community life, it becomes an individual's story that does not belong to the casteist world and is not even acceptable within his community; he is driven out of that. Here is where *Akkarmashi* deviates from other Dalit autobiographies. On speaking about this Limbale turns towards the individual self from the representation of the community when he realizes to be out of his own world into a wholly different world. He suffers the pangs of both being partitioned into the worlds of lower caste and upper castes as he says, "My father is not a Mahar by caste. In the Maharwada I felt humiliated as I was considered a bastard; they call me akkarmashi. Yet in the village I was considered Mahar and teased as the offspring of one (Limbale, 2003, 62)." He unfolds the story behind his accursed life and his throwing into the outcaste world:

> Hanmanta Limbale lured Masamai. She was given a rented house at Akkalkot, which she accepted. It was a kind of revenge to live openly with the same man who had uprooted her from her family. Hanmanta Limbale now possessed her like a pet dove. They lived happily. Masamai became a pregnant, and give birth to a son. Who's the father of this boy? Hanmanta didn't want any of this to happen, but who can disown a child? A child is a reality (Limbale, 2003, 36).

Kumud Pawade recounts a sad picture of the Sanskrit class where she has been humiliated because of her caste in "The Story of My Sanskrit" from her autobiography *Antaspot* (1981) or "Thoughtful Outburst" where she sadly expresses that wherever she goes her caste does not leave her. It is the burden of casteist politics that the Dalits have to bear throughout their lives. But, Limbale's accursed life is tantamount to a limbo. The word 'limbo' according to Collins English dictionary denotes a particular situation where people are caught between two stages and it remains unclear what will happen next. It originates to the speculative, non-scriptural doctrine of Catholic theology which shows the afterlife condition of men who die because of their 'original sin' before finally subjected to the 'Hell of the Damned'. Limbale has to bear the brunt of the sin of illegitimacy that turns his life into the edge of a living hell.

The sin committed in the consummation of his lower caste mother and the upper caste father does not permit him to live on the usual parameters of a legitimate life. Limbale expresses vengeance over his very birth: "Why didn't my mother abort me when I was a foetus? Why did she not strangle me as soon as I was born? We may be children born out of caste but does that mean we must be humiliated? What exactly is our fault? Why should a child suffer for the sin of its parents? (Limbale, 2003, 64)"

Towards the mature age of his life, he is made to live in a world that is far from the usual benchmark of caste in society. He utters out, "I was a Dalit who had become a Brahmin by attitude, but high-caste people didn't even allow me to stand at their doorsteps. Either I should live in Bhimnagar, or in the Dalit locality or even in a Muslim locality. I was an outcaste in all other localities (Limbale, 2003, 107)." He also depicts these brothers and sisters who are the equal sufferers of the shared lives of the outcaste world:

> Masamai had Nagubai, Nirmala, Vanmala, Sunanda, Pramila, Shrikant, Indira and Sridam from Kaka, whose name was Yeshwantrao Sidramappa Patil, the head of the village named Hanoor. Because they are registered as Hindu Lingayats in the official records, they are accepted neither by the Mahar community nor by the Lingayat community, so we live in a semi-Maharwada of our own (Limbale, 2003, 38).

Within both the village Maharwada and the city spaces of Sholapur, Bombay, Latur, and Bhimnagar he is ostracized to a particular societal habitat. He becomes a victim to the strategic exclusivism of the hierarchical Hindu casteist society. The burden of the illegitimate identity aids in constructing his unique outcaste world on the crucial juncture of liminality and sub-liminality.

Conclusion

This article makes an attempt to study the dilemma and consequent circumstances of fractured identity and existential crisis. *Akkarmashi* or *The Outcaste* is a narrative bildungsroman of a Dalit who is thrown out of the usual parameters of casteist paradigm. He bears within the sin of illegitimate birth and his seemingly 'impure blood' makes contested moments of afflictions and obscure existence. Throughout the journey of life, the quest for identity and subsequent transformations of social identity happen to be a foregrounding reality. There are two-fold perspectives in the narrative. On the one hand, it is the 'community autobiography' of Limbale and his Mahar community and on the other, it is an individual story of the lone sufferer who takes painstaking efforts in establishing his one and unique identity within the contested identities. The quest never ends though; it throws many questions at the end and provokes the readers to ponder over the questions again and again. Identity is a prima facie representation of a person to his own self and to the society he belongs to. However, when the identity is fractured, it creates blurred visions of representation and gives vent to such realities that are hidden underneath.

❑

Chapter-6

Voices of the Self

- Charu Arya

Introduction

Autobiographies work as the device to unveil untold incidents in the life of individual. In this rhetoric alliance of apprehensions and experiences, individual truth is placed with flow of reality. When Dalit autobiographies were beginning to find place in the literary genre at first, its purpose was to express the stigma of what a dalit goes through. Gradually, the individual narration became unanimous expression of the whole community and its suffering. Present analysis does not divide the sole narrator from his community. But what makes the distinction is the trauma that the narrator does not even belong to his own community. He was the 'Outcaste'. Here, the multi-layered suffering of the boy who was born from the womb of a dalit mother as a dalit remains unaccepted in his own caste and community. Sharankumar Limbale wrote his autobiography to angrily express his traumatic experiences from his birth as a dalit and then his struggle to survive as an outcaste. His desire was to unfold in front of everyone, untold incidents, social and caste prejudices, violence and traumatic experiences of an outcaste dalit. His aggression and rigorous questioning was meant to attack those who ostracized dalits and did atrocities on them. He also attacks manipulated use of the dominant power of upper caste to assault dalit women sexually. He is in anger while talking about fate of those children who are born out of these compelled sexual compromises and sexual atrocities. How body of dalit woman is used and thrown like garbage and garbage is then born out of that garbage! Life of that child is full of trauma where he struggles to survive fatherless and lives a life which is an abuse in itself. Sharankumar is one such child. He has used his lived experiences to raise questions. The brimming attack and showering questions on the social preachers further leads to the impact of those questions on Sharankumar himself. The questions got twisted naturally with passage of time in his life and later in the search of his own identity Sharankumar leaves many questions unanswered.

Sharankumar is in continuous struggle with the loss of identity that leads to his quest for solace within this struggle. How in the later phase of life he is searching to identify himself with identity of epic characters where divine mythical powers allow him the freedom to identify himself with their strength of being worshipped by humans. Dalit women are not only subject of sympathy for him but have also been described as wombs manufacturing fatherless children. Pain of identity-less life and struggle to survive as an *akkarmashi* is the primary analysis in *The Outcaste*.

Caste, in the social structure survives as resistance between self, identity and community. When Sharankumar Limbale expressed his traumatic experiences, he is bringing in forefront, how caste and caste identities exist amongst their caste names.

We begin with understanding meaning and the reason for the name of autobiography of Limbale, *Akkarmashi*, a Marathi word, means a person whose birth is illegitimate, impure and incomplete. This is an abuse in Marathi. Limbale in one of his interviews declares that he wanted *akkarmashi* to be the title of his autobiography because he has lived a life where his identity got defined by this word *akkarmashi*. This abuse was his identity. He was always addressed as *akkarmashi*, and this abuse was used to call his name, so, when Limbale went to the publisher, for the first time with this title, publisher wanted him to change this title to Typhoon, Cyclone or Storm which might describe his trauma better. But Limbale says it clearly that he insisted on this title, and said that what may happen, his autobiography will get published with the name that he has received from this society and it will become a radical attack back on this cruel society. He wanted to bring in open, hidden truths of life of a human child born as an *akkarmashi*. Hence, the title remained the same.

Sharankumar also describes that *akkarmashi* has another interpretation, to be described as incomplete and impure form of gold. Gold which is a metaphor of purity, pure only when it is *barah mashi*, and when we say *gyarah/akkar mashi*, it means that it is not the purest state of gold and is lesser than that which makes it impure.

Reading autobiography is different from reading Dalit autobiography. Any autobiography is born out of the urge of bringing out various episodes in life of the author, with the purpose of talking about self and experiences simultaneously whereas autobiography of a *Dalit* author becomes a medium to express experiences and the ordeal of his whole community with the expression of all others and the self. Here he feels strong enough to disclose hidden incidents and describe painful sufferings that he and his community had been experiencing for years.

Questioning Caste names and crisis of Identity

Identity crisis remained in Sharankumar's life since his birth. He was born because of the illicit relation of a Patil, an upper caste man and his mother Masamai, a dalit Mahar woman. After this, his mother was whore of another Patil, whom they called Kaka. He and his siblings, Nagi, Nirmi and Vani were born as a result of these relations.

As described in *The Outcaste*, 'There is a whole breed born to adulterous Patils. There are Dalit families that survive by pleasing the Patils sexually. The womb for most of these children was the same but the fathers were different (3).' His mother Masamai was married to Ithal Kamble, a Lingayat, and was deserted later by his father. Sharankumar was born as a result of his mother's affair with Hanmanta Limbale, a Patil. But now Sharankumar is not a Lingayat, a Patil or a Mahar. He is considered as impure and of half blood and so, was not even a Mahar (purely?). As a result, he is addressed as *akkarmashi*. The hut where, he, his sisters and his grandmother Santamai and Dada lived together was their home.

Sharankumar's mother, Masamai was deserted by her husband, Ithal Kamble because of Hanmanta Limbale, a rich man for whom Ithal Kamble had worked. Soon when Masamai was living a deserted life, Hanmanta lured her and kept her in a rented accommodation. As a result, Masamai got pregnant and gave birth to a son. And from here Sharankumar's identity crisis began. Who was his father? The one who married and left his mother or the one who enjoyed his mother sexually and as a result of these sexual connections, he was born.

Here, Sharankumar questions the birth of a child. Why the society has not made any system to identify such children? Every child born should be owned by someone. By the one who has married the mother legally or by the one who has left his seed inside the womb of the mother? He questions the purpose of being born. His anger is revealed every time he goes through the trauma of being disowned by all. He questions the most powerful system of divine world, where birth of a child cannot be considered only as the end product of sexual enjoyment or idea of survival. Rather he is questioning the existence of a child, once the child is born. He says. 'A child is a reality.'

Sharankumar's anger is not only towards the system or the person who made his mother pregnant. But now he turns his eyes towards his mother, 'Why did my mother say yes to the rape which brought me into the world? Why did she put up with the fruit of this illegitimate intercourse for nine months and nine days and allow me to grow in the fetus? Why did she allow a bitter embryo to grow?'

This question raised towards his mother makes him feel guilty to be born out of such a mother who kept an illicit relation and then gave birth to the illegitimate child. Sharankumar questions his existence every time his identity was scrutinized. His suffering increased with each instance, he could not tolerate pain of being fatherless. If somebody fought with him at home or scolded him badly, he showed his anger aggressively.

He again questioned, 'Who should I go to? Who would claim me when both my mother and father rejected me? Why didn't my mother abort me when I was a fetus? Why did she not strangle me as soon as I was born? We may be children born out of caste but does that mean we must be humiliated? What exactly is our fault? Why should a child suffer for the sin of his parents? So whenever I looked at my mother I grow wild with anger. Why did she commit adultery at all? Why shouldn't I enter my mother's bed? Isn't she an adulterous? (64)'

These poisonous thoughts of degrading his own mother were born as a result of abuses inflicted on him continuously. He was never taken care of or relieved of his pain that he was facing everyday as a fatherless and casteless child. But then when he looked at the suffering of Masamai and Santamai, he knew that they did not do this for lust but they wanted care and also there was the need to survive. They could not have been able to feed their children without exchanging their bodies for sexual usage.

And Sharankumar was agonized with the question of hunger as the strongest pain. If there would not have been hunger then these women might not have sold themselves to different men. Trauma of being fatherless and at the same time living with the mother whom he loved and hated at the same time makes him realize how he cannot go and ask his father to accept him. He knew that his mother was considered a whore. How she had to allow herself to be used sexually by the man who claimed to own her as a keep but never agreed to own the child born out of her. Why she never thought about the traumatic life her child will live. What kind of mother was she?

Sharankumar tries to imagine if his birth was treated like birth of any other child. He again questions the humiliation his mother must have faced while bearing him for nine months. He wanted to know that how his birth was celebrated, sweets distributed or naming ceremony done? These questions bring ahead the crisis he was going through in the days he started understanding how important it was to be owned by someone. To gain the identity by being born of a mother, where only she can tell who his father was? And he says. 'Whose son am I, really? (37)'

Sharankumar went through episodes of identity crisis where his birth itself was an abuse and his life hated by most as he was an illegitimate child born out of an illegitimate mother. He was annoyed, unanswered, insulted and in suffering because he could not find answers to all these questions. These questions remained and have been inducted in his autobiography to evoke the society and question the system of caste-ism:

> This is almost a tradition – a Patil, always a big landowner, has a Dalit whore. There is at least one such house in every village. Children born to such a whore have no legal father because there is an unbridgeable gap between such a father and son. The prestige of father is at stake! (58).

It was the second phase of Sharankumar's life where he was to get further education. In this phase, for the first time he realized that practically he can not move ahead without name of his father. When he went regularly to school for four to five days, the teacher wanted to register him formally. And when he was asked what his father's name was, for the first time he realized 'Strange that I too could have a father? (59)'.

This was another psychological burden for him. Till now he had hated his life and the man who got his mother pregnant illegally and he needed that same name for being legal. This super imposed identity created a chaos of need and denial at the same time. And as the whole society knew that Masamai gave birth to the child while being kept as the whore of Hanmanata Limbale, the name of Hanmanta Patil of Baslegaon was added to the school register as father of Sharankumar. For this, Hanmanta came to fight with school headmaster, Bhosale, and he also tried to threaten him, bribe him and even pleaded at the end but headmaster Bhosale refused to remove his name from the register as Sharankumar's father. And only because of him Sharankumar is carrying the surname, Limbale:

> I never wanted 'Masamai Hanmanta Limbale' named as my guardian in the official record, obviously, because Hanmanta had deserted Masamai these last eight or ten years. Now Masamai was kept by another Patil. What sort of life had she been living, mortgaging herself to one owner after another and being used as a commodity? Her lot has been nothing but the tyranny of sex (48).

Later, when the freeship form for continuing his education was to be verified by village Sarpanch, another refusal came in the path of his signing the form. The identity of Sharankumar again came under questioning. "The Sarpanch was in a real fix about how to identify me. But I too was a human being. What else did I have except a human body? But a man is recognized in this world by his religion, caste, or his father. I had neither a father's name, nor any religion, nor a caste. I had no inherent identity at all (59)."

Exploited Womb and Women Body on Sale

Sharankumar was again facing the trauma of being born from the womb of a whore. The questions that were rising in front of him were bringing him to understand that he was an unwanted child and his birth was a pain for his mother. She couldn't refuse to accept that she was a keep and as a result she will have to give birth to all the children while her owner satisfies his sexual urge. Sharankumar is also questioning the role of poverty and homelessness as strong reasons for women like his mother to provide their bodies in exchange of these essential requirements for survival. They turn blind towards understanding or realizing the trauma of that child who will be born out of these sexual favors. And they kept those doors shut till the time they actually had to face the situation themselves.

Sharankumar kept asking his mother that who was his father, really? Finally she told him that she was the Patil's whore. And that day he felt very happy, at least he finally knew what his identity was! He says, "I didn't know the meaning of the word *whore*, I thought it meant 'father'. But what a venomous word it is. It implies an impure, foul vagina. Who would willingly enter the gigantic gate of that vagina? (60)" Here, Sharankumar is not only attacking on foulness of the vagina, but he is considering vagina as the sole factor in deciding identity of both the owner of the vagina and the product of the vagina. He has called the word 'whore' venomous. It is to describe poison that is inserted in life of the woman who is a whore and has to provide her vagina every time her buyer comes to her. It is to create the reason of having vagina, which can be considered pure or impure by its user and the identity of the product born as a result of the usage of vagina.

The exchange of this venomous process begins with the need of survival. Identity at that time was not even important. The sale of vagina, brings back the basics for survival and the owner of vagina, indulges in that exchange. She, as the owner of vagina, is at the time, unable to look at the identity crisis that the product of that vagina will face. Social ownership of both the owner and the product are left on the call of the society. Sharankumar was one such product and he could never understand why his mother had to have sexual relations with all these men? He painfully argues that watching his mother doing sexual intercourse with Kaka from the gap of the door, made him dislike her more. He could not keep this thought away throughout his autobiography that how his mother could not give him the name he could have inherited. He was fatherless, despite of knowing who his father was.

In one of the incidents when Sharankumar was pushed out of community hall, later he did not go there out of fear of getting abused. He feels, "I am an alien. My father is not Mahar by caste. In the Maharwada I felt humiliated as I was considered a bastard; they called me *akkarmashi* (62)."

Trauma of many other dalit women, who went through similar treatment, bore unwanted children of men they never wanted to sleep with. In another shameful incident of a dalit girl, Dhanavva, whose husband died of lightning falling on him, returned back to her father? She was Shankar's young and beautiful daughter. Her father, Shankar, a rascal, did not attempt to remarry her and instead got her pregnant. She visited Devki, to get her child aborted. Devki, a spinster, performed abortions. But it was too late for abortion. After sexually misusing body of her own daughter, Shankar said that he had sown seed years before and now, why he should not be enjoying the fruit of it. Dhanavva kept visiting Masamai to share her pain and to cry. The agony of being sexually assaulted was commonly shared by many women around Sharankumar. Sex was one thing which was forced and remains compulsion for survival for each one of them.

Hunger and Homelessness While Struggling for Identity

How relatable it is to start believing in the power of hunger? Sharankumar has emphasized strongly in the power of hunger in his life narration. His argument began with the natural power of hunger that became a curse for him and others around him. Hunger and need to survive was the essential reason why these

The Famished Gods

women allowed sexual favors to the men from upper caste. For this Sharankumar argued that absence of hunger could have reasoned into moral acceptance of these fatherless children. He says that God gave us one stomach and different types of food. So, he questions that why God could not give us different stomachs? When man went to God and asked that there is too much to eat and drink, give me two stomachs, God replied that try and fill this one first, if you are able to fill it, then come to me and I will give you another stomach.

He saw his family surviving on leftover food for months and days. No earning, no money and no work pushed them to do every menial task coming their way. Any wedding in the village meant feast for the people of Maharwada. He describes how people from his village stayed hungry for the whole day and waited for the food that they got after all the people of upper castes have finished eating in that wedding feast.

In one of the instances, when he went to school picnic in third standard, he and his dalit friends ate the left over food given to them by their upper caste school mates. When he came back home and narrated the same to his mother, she like "a victim of famine said, Why didn't you get at least a small portion of it for me? Leftover food is nectar (3)."

Sharankumar believes hunger as the largest weakness in the life of human beings. For him, food becomes everything as a child. He is unable to think beyond hunger, minimizing everything else, family, society, friends, respect, honor or relations. He has described how he saw his little sister crying because of hunger, how his mother was angry and empty stomach always, how Santamai and Dada kept on arranging one time food for them, which was not enough to fill their empty stomach. He went running around looking for food, stole food and never felt guilty of his actions. After all it was the question of filling up their stomach.

He also went around with Santamai gathering dung and sold dried cakes of dung for little money. Santamai being the older one tried various ways and means to satisfy the hunger. During harvesting season when cattle grazed in the fields and passed undigested grains in their dung, Santamai picked up those lumps of dung and washed it in the river water to collect those grains. After drying those grains, she grind them and made *Bhakari* of it. Sharankumar could not even eat few bites of it, as it felt like eating dung itself.

Maharwada, the place where they lived was full of filthy children. "Heaps of garbage, tin sheds, dogs and pigs were our only companion (5)." Daily labor at the bus stop meant bread and butter for them. One small cup of tea was shared by three people. Dada worked as the porter in the bus stop. For small wages and with the hope that driver, conductor might share some food with Dada, Limbale says that, Hope is a strange thing. Expecting food and liquor, Dada waited till late for the last bus to halt in the night.

His description of various situations in his life, where hunger was supreme and he and his family could not think beyond it. His name, his identity all were dwarfed by hunger. Incidents of his life depict metaphorically how all was less than food. One day when the heat melted jaggery kept at the roof of the bus, he remembers how he scraped off the flakes and took it home to help through with four days of tea. But then what about tea powder? Tea bags used and strained, thrown out of tea stall of Ghenappa, were gathered by Sharankumar. They made black tea out of those tea bags and drank the concoction again and again.

The chest where *Bhakari* was stored and was eaten with curry time to time was full of cockroaches and bugs. They had to eat curry with dead cockroaches in it; they threw the cockroaches away and ate the curry.

'*Bhakari* is as large as man. It is as vast as the sky, and bright like the sun. Hunger is bigger than man. Hunger is more vast than the seven circles of hell. Man is only as big as a *bhakari*, and only as big as his hunger. Hunger is more powerful than man (50).' Mahars were informed as soon as any animal died. Boys and men went to drag the dead animal, skin it and distribute shares to others. They were addressed as 'Ox eaters! The work of cleaning the dead animals and then eating them was again a job that was decided for these lower castes and at the same time it was their social obligation and duty to clean the place of dead carcasses. Denial of this job was not taken as a positive move and the upper castes will punish them and abuse them for not fulfilling their duty. Sharankumar and his friend Parshya, many times did this job. His friend Harya one day was carrying the carcass of dead buffalo calf on his shoulder when Shobhi, a girl from the upper caste, crossed by his side. He wanted to throw that animal down and clean himself of all that bad smell coming from his body to so that she looks at him. He loved her. But he couldn't do anything else other than bringing home that dead buffalo calf and start skinning it. This was their job. Food was important for all. He kept working with tears in his dead eyes but finished his job of cleaning and chopping the pieces for cooking before he left.

Food and hunger were the highest priority for all of them. They knew if they will not work towards arranging food by doing menial jobs, killing animals and skinning them, begging, stealing or by any other means, then their people will sleep hungry.

Knowledge Enlarged Craving for Identity

Historically caste has been rooted strongly. Caste discrimination which was there in the age of Manu or may be before that did not see much dilution of castes in centuries. Caste system based on occupation of individual, divided Hindu society into different castes managing the hierarchy. Everybody stayed into a particular caste because of the occupation one had. Other than Brahmin, Khsatriya, Vaishya and Sudra, Sudras were further divided into Atisudras. The system was layered and untouchables stayed in the lowest layer. This division worked in hierarchy. Shudras born from feet of God were there to serve every other caste from their body and mind and keep them clean. As a result, the lowest polluted *varna* faced discrimination in the hands of the castes which were above in the system of caste hierarchy.

These various episodes from the text describing their untouchability, meager job conditions, struggle for bread and butter and atrocities faced by men, women and their children was all outcome of the strength that lied in the caste system. Despite of all the insult they received, no one had the courage to revolt against it otherwise, whole of Maharwada would be attacked.

In one incident, a Dalit youth made a mistake of watching with luscious eyes towards a woman from the upper caste, and when caught was beaten and Maharwada was attacked and all the dalits were imprisoned for a year. When they returned after a year, every dalit woman had a little child in her lap. They all were raped.

Caste-ism at large affected the education process of Sharankumar. After getting the surname as 'Limbale' and earning good grades in classes, he joined school at Chapalgaon for further education. He kept coming back to his village on weekends. But education could not resolve many deep - rooted issues related to his identity. Though, now with education making its way in life of Sharankumar, he was gaining strength to look beyond struggle for survival. But then his crisis of facing untouchability still left him in the state of dismay.

Separate cup plate in the small tea shop was a sign of humiliation for him and his friends. They had to leave way for others to pass, so that the 'others' do not get polluted. They lived where other people did latrine. Now that education has changed their way of thinking and looking at the society, this was further humiliation for Sharankumar. While in their own village discrimination and untouchability was a normal practice with people of their community.

This was another phase in the life of Sharankumar where he started questioning caste-ism and practice of untouchability. With education he earned some courage to question the system of caste where human beings are treated as if they are worst than animals. Division in *Varna system* led to considering Mahars as the lowest category and dead animal eaters, they could not eat food, drink water, earn wages, make property or marry them. Atrocities against Dalits was part of routine life, they were held responsible, tied to pole and beaten if any animal was found dead in the village, Dalit women if went close to the farms of upper caste to graze their animals, they were abused and shouted and kicked off. There were many women and girls who were sexually assaulted and even raped in these crop fields. This history of atrocities can be heard in the stories of Santamai.

The level of frustration increasing inside him and lack of identity despite of education led him and many others to adopt radical methods. Sharankumar and his friends made complaint in the police station against discrimination of plates and cups at the tea shop, they went inside the temple and prostrated in front of God, they also drank water from the well that belonged to Patil's but was constructed by Mahars.

Desiring Solutions in Correlation with Divine and Historical Heroes

After all these years of suffering and questioning his own existence along with rigorous efforts for survival, now we find Sharankumar looking for solutions in the divine and spiritual world. His inspiration to resist his further suffering lies now in what he has been educated about ideals and heroes. Further his struggle lies in finding his identity while mirroring himself with powerful historical figures and divine heroes. Sharankumar now believed that his agony is agony of Lord Buddha and he searched Buddha for peace and equality. He knew that Buddha will arouse in him. This also connects with Bhimrao Ambedkar and his faith in Buddha. How he finally raised himself above caste identity to the identity in Buddhism. He also became restless listening to the painful history of dalits and felt the same restlessness that Shivaji felt.

Whenever he heard that the reservation of lower castes will be finished, he was scared, that how they will complete their education, he says give us our Dalitsthan! The questions kept coming back to him even when he finished his education and got a job at *Latur* in the telephone department and married to Kusum, an eighteen year old girl. He went back to his people and still saw there was too much that needs to be questioned and changed.

There were times when his questions made him realize that his mother was not less than *Kunti* of *Mahabharata*. And he could identify himself as *Karna*, son of *Kunti*, born before her marriage. He was always considered as her illegitimate son and she could never give him the identity he deserved. *Karna* was considered as *Surya- putra*, born as a result of seed sown by God *Surya* in the womb of *Kunti* when she was unmarried. *Karna* was left floating in a basket in the river to meet his fate. After this and throughout the epic, he could not live the privileged and respectful life of a child born out of a royal mother, that privilege was enjoyed by other children born out of the womb of same mother. They had father, who owned them. Sharankumar could relate with him because he was also living the life of *Karna*, where he knew he will just have to follow the flow of the river. He knew he will remain disowned.

This comparison of himself with *Karna* is providing Sharankumar two ways of finding answers to the questions of identity crisis that he was facing. Firstly, he now has the answer to consider his mother as a woman who has been part of this divine world in the epic that has been celebrated with the existence of Gods in it. He was still unable to express the trauma his mother must have gone through in carrying the child within her when the whole society was raising questions on her credibility as a mother. He found solace in shadowing his mother's life with life of *Sita* and *Kunti*. He feels that the trauma of his mother subsided as soon as he was born. And he and *Karna* both started suffering as soon as they were born.

Secondly, he has now, *Karna*, with whom he could connect and stand close. A child, born in the similar circumstances, fatherless, identity less and a child who struggles to complete the incompleteness in his life. He is struggling with finding his identity when he knows no one will come forward to own him or even if he fights for it he will not be able to earn it. And he with this comparison is fulfilling his desire of finding some identity and he finds it in identifying himself with *Karna*.

Sharankumar could identify himself with *Karna, Lord Budha* and *Shivaji*; they all existed within him in different phases of his life that he lived as an *akkarmashi*. Even at the end of his autobiography, he says that he was not comfortable to reveal to people that he was actually fatherless, an *akkarmashi*. His autobiography is a painful journey into his stigmatic experiences of being fatherless, a bastard born out of a whore. And he has not denied that he existed and also accepted himself as *akkarmashi*, the Outcaste!

Dalit should write dalit literature. So, he says that the way he cannot write literature on women, despite of all his efforts because he cannot feel the pain that a woman goes through. It was urgent for him to bring it in front of the whole world, life of an *akkarmashi* from the mouth of an *akkarmashi*.

There is a debate today, that the mainstream writers have been asking dalits to come in the mainstream writings, and for that Limbale says, 'From centuries our homes are away from mainstream, our food, our language every thing has always been kept away from mainstream then why today you have issues with Dalit Literature being written separately?

❑

Chapter-7

Layers of Resistance

- Yasmeena Jan

Dalits are the broken people who are excluded from the fourfold Varna system of Hinduism. They are also called untouchables because the upper castes use to consider them as polluted beings. The synonymous terms used for Dalits are scheduled castes, scheduled tribes and other backward classes. This community lives all over India having different languages and cultures. According to Dalit Panthers, "Dalit is no longer merely an untouchable outside the village walls and the scripture. He is untouchable and he is a Dalit, but he is also a worker, a landless laborer, a proletarian (Joshi 141-42)." Majority of the Dalits are in South India. After the Independence, India introduced a reluctance organization to enlarge the potential of Dalits to have political depiction in order to acquire government jobs and education. They face discrimination at every level in their day to day life. Menial jobs like cleaning toilets, sweeping and garbage throwing are meant for them. They have to feed upon the leftovers and fight with the animals for food. The word Dalit is itself a beautiful word as it has embraced the terms like oppression, subjugation, and exploitation in itself. It thus refers to the deplorable state or condition, to which a large group of people have been reduced by social, economic, religious, and political conventions in which they are living. Arjun Dangle the prominent Dalit leader defines Dalits as:

Dalit means masses exploited and oppressed economically, socially and culturally in the name of religion and other factors. Dalit writers hope that this group of people will bring about revolution to the country (*Poisoned Bread*, 65).

The unique journey of Dalits seemed to be beginning in the 1970's. Waharu Sonavane, an Adivasi poet, was a protester observant from the beginning to edifying ending but by the late 1980's these were appropriate principal themes, as he impaired the control of non-tribal in Adivasi-based activities. He happened to assert that the Adivasis who had been disrupted by religious norms and supporting parties ought to approach together. The 1980's were obvious not only by the pronouncement of Dalits and other low castes, but also by the ascend of other new social activities of farmers combating beside their mistreatment by the market and states, of tribal and caste Hindu peasants fraught in opposition to upbringing destruction and disarticulation. These arrangements began to recognize at least in part- at the beginning- with a critique of Hinduism and to put forth new edifying themes that began to bring together with those of the Dalit anti caste social order. An eminent writer Anandhi S. writes, "Dalit reflects caste- based identities which continue to remain the fundamental identities of people (54)." By late 1980's, Dalit and other low caste women from south India were also building themselves visible. They tried to retrieve non-Aryan and anti-Brahmin civilization, taking Sita as a conception of development rather than an ideal, and asserted that the Ramayana that described the success of patriarchy seemingly in excess of matriarchy.

The rationale of Dalit policy emerged as a grievance to the very explanation of Hinduism as the preponderance over religion and the derivation of Indian institution; an assertion that it was a Brahminic Hinduism that portrayed the hegemony of a majestic above that tradition, and this supremacy had to subsist over terrified. Dalits themselves have a propensity to include all the sections of the subjugated, demoralized and marginalized by the social group exploitation, counting Adivasis, and further backward classes, women and oppressed nationalities. Dalit inscription is a blend of new profitable and supporting route with the cultural prosecutes. Dalits and all additional marginalized people have been progressively affirmed themselves- but often at cross purposes, often smooth in resentment to one another. Dalits had constantly

The Famished Gods

seen Gandhism as simply a supplementary complex explanation of Hindutva; after all, heavy and further more startling anti Muslim riots in Gujarat, the centre of Gandhi's ability, seemed toward proving that the Hindutva Ram raj was merely a step missing from Gandhi's Ram raj. Baburao Bagul, an honor appealing author and one time Marxist party member, had in printing denounced the domination of Hindu image in the general association. He asserted that in independence and the bourgeois insurgency had a residential and progressive content, and people had fought religious enthusiasts, but in India, xenophobia was strolled into a form of traditional worship. Bagul went on to argue that since Hindus are the mainstream, there was a reticent hope for from the Indian practice. Egalitarian collectivism is based on emancipation while impartiality and union is the view point of the modern age. And this thinking has its basis in the Indian consciousness and numinous worth-structure.

The writing of the saints has not supported any meaningful choice in the forms of ideals. On the supplementary, fascism, yearning ascendancy, hero-worship, arrogance, disdain, malice and loathing- all these have unyielding legendary and intellectual support. Dalit politics made a precious swiftness in the 1980's and 1990's, foremost it was indeed a major alternative to the arousal of Hindutva. In the 1980's, the supporting alternatives promising from the new social movements remained a failure. But, by the end of the decade, an innovative pool was approaching forward, The Bahujan Samaj Party. This was the latest verbalization of Dalit supporting force, but its propel was to be an unconventional one. Dalits face discrimination at every level as they are not allowed to eat with other caste members. They are forced to face social discrimination by upper castes when they refuse to perform their duties. In this regard, Gopal Guru writes, "The body of the Dalits is treated as if it is trapped into a septic tank even if it is a vibrant think tank. This is obnoxiously special to the Indian form of reduction (213)." Dalit children face discrimination in schools also. They are not allowed to drink water from the same source. They belong to the neglected class and this do not form a class of their own. Thus, they are the ignored people in the Indian society. Defending the Indian caste system, Gandhi writes, "...Caste does not cannote superiority or inferiority. It simply recognizes different outlooks and corresponding modes of life… (174-75)."

Dalit literature is the literature written by both Dalits and Non-Dalits about the lives of the oppressed group of people living in India. This writing forms a significant element of Indian literature. Dalit writing emerged in 1960's in Maharashtra and subsequently flourished within supplementary parts of India, through narratives such as poems, short stories, novels and autobiographies. The origin of this writing can subsist backside to Buddhist literature; Dalit Bhakti poets like Gora, Raidas, Chokha Mela and Karmamela, and the Tamil Siddhas, several of which must have been Dalits going by hagiographical balance sheet like Periyapuranum. Autonomous and classless thinkers such as Narayana Guru, Jyotiba Phule, Dr. B.R. Ambedkar, articulated the modes of how repression on the basis of caste needs to be understood through modern Dalit literature so that it can be brought to notice for its sublimation. It was in 1958 when the term Dalit literature was used at the first conference of Maharashtra Dalit Sahitya Sangha in Mumbai. It was Namdeo Dhasal, the originator of Dalit Panthers Movement whose writings cemented conduct for the strengthening of Dalit literature. It was in 1993, Ambedkar Sahitya Parishad, Wardha structured the first Akhil Bharatiya Ambedkari Sahitya Sammelan in Wardha, Maharashtra to enroute for re-conceptualize and to renovate Dalit Sahitya. After the name of Dalit modern age hero, researcher and encouragement who has campaigned alongside the caste prejudice and was a physically powerful promoter of Dalit privileges. Arjun Dangle disconnected this literature as:

> Dalit literature is one which acquints people with the caste system and Untouchability in India…. It matures with a sociological point of view and is related to the principles of negativity, rebellion and loyalty to science, thus finally ending as revolution (*Poisoned Bread*, 319).

Dalits are marginalized in the Indian caste-ridden society. They started writing after being silenced for centuries. They revolted against social injustices done to them in their writings. Dalit writers always hope for the society devoid of discrimination and injustice. There were a majority of writers, who started writing about the pain, sorrows, and grief. The writers whose writings became popular were as: Namdeo Dasal, Daya Pawar, Arjun Dangle, Basudev Sunani, Imayam, Mangal Rathod, Sharankumar Limbale, Jyotiba Phule and S.M. Mate. Many of these writers wrote poetry, short stories, autobiographies and novels. These writers portrayed the realistic picture of Dalits in their writings. Most of the writers of this genre wrote autobiographies, in which they explicate their own sufferings as well as the sufferings of the whole community. The most commonly read Dalit autobiographies were Laxman Manes' *Upara*, Sharankumar Limbale's *The Outcaste*, Omprakash Valmiki's *Joothan*, and Daya Pawar's *Baluta*. Dalit writers expressed their sorrows, feelings and anguish in their self-narratives very well. According to Dalit writer Sharankumar Limbale, Dalit literature is "...Marked by a sense of community, sharing, warmth, and physicality but often wretched (Limbale 14)." In an interview by Jaydeep Sarangi, Limbale well ascertains the development of Dalit writings and liberates it from the set notions:

JS: Do you consider Dalit writing as the corpus of pain and suffering?

Sharan: No...no...this is half truth. In the first stage of Dalit literature, there is corpus of pain and suffering. In this stage cry is the main theme. In 1960's, the main tone was pain. Dalit writers were writing about their sufferings and asking the world at large about humanity... our blood and your blood is red. Why are you destroying us? When the young writers started to write, they straightaway started to reject this brutal social system. In this stage pain became secondary and problem became a bullet... in the third stage, we started to revolt against injustice. The rebellious mood became important tone of our expression. So, Dalit literature is not only corpus of pain and suffering, but it is revolt against inhumanity (Limbale Int. *Poet Crit* 40).

Autobiography as a variety is the mainly utilized and the most translated genre in Dalit literature. Autobiographies are the most appropriate for studying voices. They don't deal with the growth of a single protagonist as in case of conventional autobiographies. They shift between the personal and the communal 'I' and 'we'. It is due to this fact, that this genre like the novels has been able to accommodate a plethora of voices within a single text. Hence the scope for poly vocality is produced. Most of the Dalit autobiographies are written in regional languages and then translated into English. Autobiography as a genre is rarely practiced by Indians as compared to that of poetry and fiction. It problematized the most important issues of caste, class and gender in the Indian milieu. Apart from recovering an individual's discovery of selfhood and contention of distinctiveness, it also offers a background portrait of the Indian culture, counting interpersonal and inter-communal relations, clashes and tolerances. The present study highlights the autobiographical elements in Sharankumar Limbale's autobiographical novel *The Outcaste*. It is the true representation that portrays a Dalit life. This book has attracted the attention of all who are interested in Subaltern studies. It narrates the story of narrator's childhood experiences as an Untouchable born in Indian society.

Sharankumar Limbale born on June 1, 1956 is a poet and fictional critic. He has written large number of books and is known for his autobiography *Akkarmashi* (*The Outcaste*). This book is translated into many languages. The English version of this book is available by the Oxford University Press as *The Outcaste*. His important work *Towards an Aesthetics of Dalit Literature* is painstaking among the most essential works on Dalit literature. According to Sharankumar Limbale, in the book *The Outcaste*, the caste of a person determines his uniqueness, counting the clothes he will wear, the human being he may tie the knot and the food stuff he will eat. The raconteur of the book describes the life of a gentleman who suffered the pain of caste structure. This novel was foremost written in Marathi in 1984. In this book, Sharankumar Limbale portrayed the despondent days he lived as an outcaste, as a half caste, and as an impecunious man. *Akkarmashi* was translated into English by Santosh Bhoomkar in 2003. *The Outcaste* is regarded as impenetrable family in common and community fights back scrupulously. It sees the situation of a particular marginalized class, namely Mahar community. This book portrays the accurate representation of the darker side of the Indian social order. The only way to find out the embarrassment of the Dalits and other subjugated sections is in the course of the manner and emotions of those who have lived throughout the skills and who have the education and ability to inscribe such illustration about it. One such foundation is Sharankumar Limbale's autobiography *The Outcaste*. He has also printed numerous short stories and novels on Dalit life, tribulations and fight. He used a personal description style in his autobiography to represent the life experiences of a Dalit which includes inequality, discrimination, and indifferences towards them and their culture. The author thinks to see his painful situation of not having his individual identity, a home or place of belonging.

Sharankumar was born as an unlawful child of a superior caste Patil and a poor landless invulnerable mother. As a route of which Sharankumar Limbale neither belonged to Mahar society nor of the Maratha caste; he is an akkarmashi, an outcaste. His mother lived in a hut, and his father in a citadel. Hence the son was against the law. Due to this reason, he could not get most of the papers signed for school and the school teachers would not extravagance his grandmother as his custodian because she lived with a Muslim and meant for apparent disagreement they might not acknowledge his last name since it belongs to an upper caste. When it was time for matrimony, he could not even get married to a low caste girl since his blood was not pure; he was not conventional at any place with public or teachers. Even a drunkard who had given Limbale his daughter would not allow her to abscond after the nuptials because of Limbale's identity. Due to this broken identity the protagonist suffered his complete life. Sharankumar remarks by winning his own splintered identity in following words as:

> My father and his forefathers were lingayat. Therefore I am one too. My mother was Mahar. My mother's father and forefathers were Mahar, hence I am a Mahar. From the day I was born until today, I was brought up by my grandfather Mahmood Dastagir Jamadar. My grandfather lives with my grandmother, Shantamai. Does this mean I am a Muslim as well? How can I be high caste when my mother is untouchable? If I am an untouchable; what about my father who is high caste? I am like Jarasandh. Half of me belongs to the village, whereas the other half is excommunicated. Who am I? To whom is my amblical cord connected? (*Akkarmashi*, 38-39)

Nevertheless, his incredible power and bravery, he did not consent to these collectively construct defenses to stop him from getting an edification and in due course publishing his story. Dalits lived outside huts, peripheral to the villages which expose their arrangement. Concerning the house, Sharankumar asserts that the bus stand was akin to home. Dalits lay like superfluous bus tickets, and they were totally reliant on the upper caste society. They ate surplus food, did inferior work, and wore clothes not needed by upper class social order. It is said that for gratifying stomachs men became thieve and women became whores. However, due to the miserable life situations, Sharankumar goes to the degree of maxim that God had made a mistake of bountiful stomachs to the Dalits. The situation of the untouchables is such that they smidgen, beg, sort grain from dung, carry deceased animals and eat them in order to pacify their desire. In the case of social order, Brahmins were the highly developed ones, then the Kshatriyas, and then the Vaishyas and Shudras. The fifth which was not as part of the caste system were Dalits. The unkindness reached its heights when the Dalits were enforced with massacre, rape and many more such like allegations. Inclined by people like Shahu, Phule, Gandhiji and Ambedkar, Dalit writers in progress have emphasized on their accessible issues. Following the way of leaders, Dalit writers began writing, focusing on themes such as unpleasantness on Dalits, social equality and economic democracy.

Ambedkar influenced the writings of Dalits; he himself was a Dalit who became a social activist, skilled and the separatist organizer of Dalits in India. Following the lane of Ambedkar, Dalits in progress challenging equality, which was unacceptable to the higher castes? Dalit literature represents the commanding talented drift in the Indian literary field. Dalit literature began as an influence of protestation against an unfair social order. It reflects the predicament of the marginalized community of the world, and highlights the struggles of human courage against the age old subjugation next to them. The issues connected to Dalit women have been taken up treacherously moreover by political privileged or the scholars in recent times. Dalit women were the Dalits among Dalits. Sharankumar Limbale portrays the pitiable and despondent life of a poor and under enemy control residents in his works in a very exceptional style. In *The Outcaste*, Sharankumar Limbale uncovered a world of poverty in addition to injustice in which the Dalits had lived for thousands of years. Autobiographical writings are tolerably found in Dalit literature which had a noteworthy anxiety on society as it depicts first hand experiences. Dalit literature is not a minimalist literature, it is connected by means of movement in the direction of transport about a change. Dalits face operation efficiently, socially and culturally in the name of belief and other factors. Dalit writers like Sharankumar Limbale anticipate that this group of people will bring in a socio-instructive insurrection in India.

Autobiography has become a significant field to communicate the bitter understanding of Dalits humiliation and inequality in India. The medium of autobiography is the most appropriate genres of studying voices. Dalit writers construct use of autobiographies by which they can allocate personal experiences of caste unfairness, making its subsistence incontestable for the middle classes. In Dalit autobiographies, authors' experiences are meant to illustrate the experiences of the community. The plots are strung mutually by a series of throbbing incidents that are outcome of the humiliation they face. Dalit autobiographies do not only correspond to the positive future of the individual but also of the community as well. The self in Dalit autobiographies is both sociologically and historically constituted. It is this normative connection between the individual and the community that empowers Dalits to offer unbiased criticism of community practices.

The Outcaste portrays the most humiliated events and insults which Limbale and his whole family underwent in different places. *The Outcaste* is the story of exploitation, humiliation, marginalization and victimization of the narrator and his community. The writer exposes the bitter reality and war against the injustices done towards Dalits in his autobiography. He narrates the episode of pain when he remembered his school picnic. It was a bitter experience for him. The narrator and other Dalit classmates were busy in playing the game of touch and go. When the upper caste boys and teachers finished eating their delicious dishes, they asked the Dalits to collect the leftovers. Sharankumar was himself an untouchable and thus is rebuked by his mother when he returns home for not bringing some of the leftovers for the rest of the family to taste. When the narrator goes to school the next day, the teacher asked him to write an essay about the picnic day. The teacher shouted at him like this, 'you son of bitch, come on, start writing! You like eating an ox, don't you'? (4) Sharankumar could not write anything because he was confused. He can only remember how the upper castes offered Dalits the leftover food and the damaged tree in whose shade Dalits are forced to take rest. This shows the exploitation of Dalits by both the upper castes as well in the hands of teachers also. It has been a tradition for non-Dalit teachers and students in India to harass, marginalize, and insult the Dalit students. Dalits are forced to a level where they can hardly dream of themselves. Sharankumar Limbale also narrates the humiliation of Dalits in the Teli mansion also. When the narrator along with other Dalit students was sitting there, an upper caste noticed them and snatched the bags of all of them. It was unbearable for the narrator. This was what Dalits have to face in their daily life. The upper caste boys throw stones at narrator and teased him by calling 'Mahar'.

Sharankumar narrates his experience at the wedding at Hanoor where the Dalit boys and Dalit girls are treated as animals. When the upper caste people started eating food, they uttered the names of Gods and saints. There the narrator wanted to eat more and though his stomach was full. Giving plate full of kheer the narrator starts walking towards his home. When an upper caste man saw him he snatches his plate and throws it on the ground. Sharankumar then utters the bitter experience at the wedding feast in the following lines:

They served the kheer in our plates very young children were given only a small portion. I ate greedily as soon as I was served and emptied my plate I asked for more helpings. As Masomai was alone at home and hungry, I thought of sneaking the delicacy to her. I asked for more and more kheer though my stomach was full and walked back home with it. I was very happy at what I was doing. But Girmallya happened to notice me. He snatched my bowl of kheer, throws it to the ground and slapped me in the face. Son of a bitch he shouted. If you didn't want it then why you have taken it? Don't let me see you more than once at any feast after this. The scum! They eat as much as they want and still crave for more to take home. I returned home crying. Girmallya didn't allow anyone to sneak the kheer away. That included my sister too. I returned home with my empty plate but Shantamai had managed to sneak some kheer away (8-9).

The Famished Gods

The above lines show how Dalits are treated and humiliated badly by the upper caste people. Sharankumar also narrates his own experience at high school Chungi. His own village school was only upto seventh class standard. In order to get admission in the village school nearby, he has to fill up the admission form with the signature of parents and village head. From beginning Sharankumar puts his own thumb impression in place of parent's signature but the signature of the village head was always a problem for the narrator. At the secondary school record, the narrator does not want to write the name – Masamai Hanmanta Limbale – as a guardian in the official record. As Masamai had left by Hanmanta from the last ten years, she was kept then by another Patil as a whore. The village head remains always in confusion of knowing the real father of Sharankumar. It was the Guruji who asked the village head to sign up his form. It was a very bitter experience for him, being annoyed the narrator said: "Has anyone seen who sowed his seeds? Has anyone seen the intercourse of his parents that resulted in his birth? (61)" It was at the age of eleven or twelve when he suffered a lot of humiliation in the hands of upper caste people. When he goes to submit his application form, he faced the following questions from his teacher: "Do you have no father? He replied, no! He is dead. The teacher also asked him, do you have no mother? He replied, no she too is dead? (62)" The teacher being aware of all of this asked these questions in order to confess him his identity of being inferior. After he completed his school education, he got admission in Dayanand College, Sholapur. He felt free in the new environment there. But he was hurted when a clerk in a college enquired about his caste and religion. His quest for identity also began to hurt him when he asserts this like:

I was afraid of my caste because I could not claim my father's caste and religion. I a sense I was not a Mahar, because high caste because high caste blood ran in my body. My own body nauseated me. The agony I lived through is my own as much as of that my village. The life of my village was mine. I was wounded by this Landlord's mansion (82).

Sharankumar completed his education at Chungi and Chapalgaon. His grandmother used to come to him with a pair of broken chapals. As they were broken from the front side, she had gone to cobbler, who was at bus-stand and repaired old chapals.

When she asked to repair this chapal, the cobbler refused to do so, as he recognized her as Mahar. This was also a bitter incident for narrator but he could not take any action. He also remembers the time when the animals died in village, the villagers accused Dalits of having poisoned them. They tied the Dalits to pole and beat them like animals. All the men and women were beaten badly. The narrator remembered his life where he had to live with the members of his own community. Being influenced by Ambedkar, he started to speak "Jay Bhim" instead of Namaskar.

It was for the first time that he revolted against oppression. The narrator not only suffered in the hands of upper caste men but also in the hands of his own community. Both Dalits and non-Dalits have subjected him to a level of extreme oppression, suffering and humiliation. He narrates one such incident in which his mother-in-law insults him. She told him, "There is no discipline in your house... we won't send our daughter until you are independent. Don't treat her like wife. ...now that you are married, sleep with her at once and prove that you are a man (100)." Injustice and humiliation faced by the narrator is not present phenomenon but a phenomenon of long tradition. Through education, the protagonist understands the new meaning of self-identity, humiliation and injustice. He was awakening under a new consciousness which was becoming attractive and supplementary day by day. It was during these circumstances that he meets his past love Shevanta. She serves as an inspiration for him to fight against the patriarchal caste ridden Hindu society. It is in this way; the narrator grows up like Karna and makes self-identity in his own mind.

Akkarmashi: The Outcaste, a text devised to delineate the trauma of a community sidelined since ages, is factually a worth reading text which allows the readers not to buy several aspects of a compelling life. The author's best part evident in the text admist layers of resistances described through numerous incidents in his phlegmatic disposition towards myriad piercing situations is his composure that becomes a fantastic example. It is also important to see how the writer translates T.S. Eliot's theory of 'Objective Correlative' while depicting catastrophic events close to his own life. It is a phenomenal text which opens many doors to a world which, needless to speak, can bring a concord among the common mass beyond all differences of opinion and stratum.

❑

Chapter-8

Re-inscribing the Cultural Ambit

- Dr. Binu K D

- Anne Placid

Introduction

Caste is the inescapable determinant of identity formation of an individual in India. The ideological and cultural practices of caste system had an all-pervasive effect on the Dalits. They were treated as contemptible and were exploited and denied of their basic human rights for several millennia. But the cultural oppression of Dalits, with its far reaching repercussions, was far more dehumanizing than their economic deprivation. The denial of Dalits' access to material resources was complemented by the robbing off their subjectivities. The dominant castes contrived it by imposing on them the stigma of pollution thus depriving them of any scope of dignity and self-expression. Through their discursive practices, the dominant castes strove to achieve the agenda of reproducing the ideology of caste and interpreting the identities of the oppressed Dalits. In this way, Dalits were excluded from the realm of culture and representation.

Dalit writing offers to counter this epistemological violence by deconstructing the stereotypical representations of Dalits in 'Dalitist' (Dalit+elitist) discourses and constructing an alternative discourse. The chapter interrogates how Sharankumar Limbale's *Akkarmashi*, translated as *The Outcaste* (2003), offers a critique on the elite cultural discourse and tries to put forth an alter/counter cultural discourse. It also attempts to analyse how Limbale's narrative re-inscribes the cultural ambit of Dalits from an insider's perspective. Along with their struggle to gain control over material resources, Dalits also struggle over the socially constructed meanings, definitions and identities.

The Outcaste and the Genre of Autobiography

Dalit autobiography marks an epistemological shift as it radically breaks away from the traditions and conventions of mainstream Indian autobiographies as well as their western counterparts. Autobiography as a literary genre emerged in the west as a product of Enlightenment project (Pascal 2). It exemplifies the individual's attempts to construct a unified self by the "shaping of the past, imposing a pattern on life and constructing a coherent self out of the fragments of experience" (ibid 9). As Linda Anderson observes, even many of the Twentieth century Autobiographies uphold the essentialist or romantic view of self hood, generated at the close of the eighteenth century, that "each individual possesses a unified, unique selfhood which is also the expression of a universal human nature (5)." Consistent with the project of Modernity their narrative always emphasizes a linear-world view, reflecting the Modernist perception of history as a continuous progression and development of human society. The autobiographical narratives of mainstream Indian writers toe the line of European models owing to the colonial legacy. Colonialism influenced their perception of time, history, culture and political thinking, significantly. Therefore, autobiography in India, as a narrative genre, reinforces the view of self as a 'knowable' rational entity constituted in terms of individual's achievements and personal politics. It represents the self as an interior territory - the private domain - distanced from the public domain and its social and political environment. Gandhiji's *The Story* of *My Experiments with Truth* is a suitable example where one comes across even the private moorings of his self. His auto-narrative unveils the most personal and innermost realms of his experience endeavouring to realize his "true" self.

Dalit autobiography reverses the above notion of autobiography as a narrative of exclusive private domain of the individual. In this regard, noted writer and critic E.V. Ramakrishnan's observation is pertinent: "It — Dalit autobiography — problematizes the relation between the society and the individual and the private and the public by conceiving of the self not merely in private or personal terms (99)." Dalits have been historically essentialized into silence.

The Famished Gods

So the attempt of Dalit writer is to reclaim Dalit voices. Since Dalit as outcaste is excluded from the realms of cultural and historical representations, the endeavour in Dalit writings especially in Dalit life writings is to re-inscribe Dalit cultural and historical consciousness relying on Dalits' collective memory. Hence, in Dalit autobiographies one finds traces of Dalit culture and history as memories. Expression of Dalit self demands new modes of narration and signification, as it does not deal with a unified and coherent 'knowable' self but a divided, fragmented 'unscruitable' self or 'non-self'. The divided and degraded Dalit self or selves is the locus of expression in Limbale's pioneering work *The Outcaste*.

The Philosophical Bedrock of Dalit Life Writing

The goal of Dalit Literature is the emancipation of the Dalits, who have been, for centuries, subjugated to the hegemony of caste. Though there are many causes for the emergence of Dalit Literature in the Twentieth century, the primary cause behind it is Dr B.R. Ambedkar. Ambedkar is now remembered as the chief draftsman of Indian constitution. But towering this, he was a great champion of Dalits cause. Dalit literature evolved as an offshoot of the political mobilisation of untouchables initiated by Ambedkar against the injustice meted out to them. He exhorted them to 'educate, agitate and organize'. His independent and autonomous mobilisation of Dalits was aimed at attaining equal status with caste Hindus in all walks of life. According to Ambedkar this goal could be achieved only by accomplishing the daunting task of caste annihilation because he considered caste as the main hindrance to Dalits' social emancipation. He said "Caste is the monster that crosses your path. You cannot have political reforms; you cannot have economic reforms, unless you kill this monster (Narasaiah, 7)." Ambedkar also realized that Dalits can never achieve equality with caste Hindus unless they are politically empowered. Therefore, he demanded separate electorates for Dalits. Although the British had accepted his demand, Gandhiji staunchly opposed it as he considered it to be a ploy by the British to divide Hindu society and he undertook a fast unto death. Finally, Ambedkar had to compromise sacrificing Dalit interests which ultimately resulted in the Poona Pact.

Ambedkar's commitment to the cause of Dalit empowerment and his social and political movement for their democratic civil rights were capable of galvanizing Dalits and they instilled in Dalits a sense of self-respect and self-pride. Dalit literature was the visible expression of this new spirit and enlightenment ignited by Ambedkar. Dalit writer consciously espouses a Dalit identity in a resolve to destroy oppressive caste system and attempts to rebuild the society based on the democratic principles promulgated by Ambedkar. Since Dalit Literature pledges itself to the Ambedkar's ideology, it is bound to be different from the mainstream writings.

As a new literary genre with an evident disregard for form, content and style, Dalit Literature discredits both the Western and Eastern literary theoretical formulations. Evidently, Dalit autobiography discounts and discredits the dominant autobiographical discourse and its narrative tropes. As a discursive subaltern genre, it articulates the lived experiences in stark realistic manner, bearing the imprint of the blood and tears of the oppressed in the vernacular. The very language, idiom, images and symbols spring from experiences instead of observations on life. Limbale pertinently differentiates Dalit Literature as literature of *Anubhava* (Experience) from non-Dalit literature as literature of *Anumana* (Imagination or speculation).

Exposition of Dalit Consciousness

Dalit life writings voice the concerns of Dalits; their shared experiences of caste oppression and untouchability and the need for a collective struggle against oppressive power structures. This feeling of shared identity or identitarianism constitutes Dalit consciousness. In the view of Limbale as expressed in his book *Towards an Aesthetic of Dalit Literature*, "Dalit Literature is the writings about Dalits with a Dalit consciousness (9)." *The Outcaste* exhibits a spirit reluctant to be vanquished by the traumatic life experiences which instead turns it to an impetus to fight the odds of life. Limbale does not yield to the 'wretched' existence of his community but obtains social mobility by liberating himself from caste bondage through education. Like Ambedkar the knowledge he acquired through education guided him to think differently. His imbibing of Dalit Consciousness, an understanding of their shared historic experiences of exclusion, subjugation, dispossession and oppression down the ages liberates him. Limbale expresses this consciousness in the most unambiguous terms in *The Outcaste*.

The Famished Gods

Having dealt elaborately with his pain and the sufferings of his community, Limbale locates the root cause of them in the caste system and proclaims his determination to fight against it, "All this is because we are controlled by caste. We are the vanquished. We are fighting another battle against convention. Though we may be defeated in this, there will be yet another battle in which we never surrender (91-92)." The 'outcastes' of history who are rendered voiceless and relegated as passive objects in 'Dalitist' (Dalit+elitist) at once assume a voice and agency in Limbale's autobiography. What makes this transformation is the influence of Ambedkarite thought. Limbale narrates the change that he undergoes after he comes in contact with the mind stirring ideas of Ambedkar, "I stopped saying 'namaskar' and started saying 'Jai Bhim' instead. . . . My youth had assumed a new meaning and significance. The blood flowed like hot lava through my body. My mind burned with myriad thoughts in silent protest. Babasaheb filled me with reverence. I felt I was meeting my mother of the last seven births (86)."

Autobiography has been a favoured genre of writers, ever since the inception of Dalit Literature, for the unequivocal expression and assertion of Dalit consciousness. According to Limbale "That literary work is the best which raises the highest degree of Dalit consciousness (*Towards an Aesthetic of Dalit Literature* 113)." His own autobiography eloquently epitomizes this.

Community - Self Equilibrium

Maintaining a symmetrical relationship between self and society is the main challenge in articulation of Dalit consciousness. Through *The Outcaste* what Limbale provides is not just a realistic account of his life as a Dalit for what he says can be extended to the life of any individual of Mahar community. While the narrator's self reflects particularly his life as an outcaste, he also ponders over the pitiable plight of his people in general. The construction of the self through narration in relation to one's caste identity is a unique feature of Dalit autobiography. While articulating the concerns of Dalit self, the narration does not become "self-centric" as in mainstream autobiographical narratives. In a Dalit life, writing the conflicts of the self becomes a paradigm for representing the conflicts of the community as an expansion of the self itself. The "I" in Limbale's book that stands for the author-narrator is inextricably linked with "we" representing the Dalit community. The narrative often oscillates between the individual 'I' and the collective 'We' as in this passage, "Our village has provided us with bread, so we owe much to them. They did provide bread but in exchange satisfied their lust with our women. I can bear to think of Masami caught between bread and lust (64)." The narrator-protagonist's identity finally coalesces with the collective identity of the community as in the following passage, "what a miserable past we lived! My agony was not limited to myself alone. Injustice done to me was not just today's phenomenon but had a long history. The roots of this injustice went deep into history, for many thousands of years (79)."

In mainstream life writings, the individual is located in a conflict ridden relationship with society, where as in Dalit life writing, both exist in harmonious rapport with each other. Though Limbale consistently employs the first person narrator, it is the third person point of view i.e. the perspective of the community that ultimately prevails. The text brilliantly validates the transformation of a disempowered caste subaltern to a speaking subject, a writer who expresses not just his individual voice, but also the collective voice of his community. In this regard Limbale's work is more of an ethno-biography than an autobiography.

In *The Outcaste*, Limbale voices equal concern for the out-caste-ness of his self as well as the 'wretched' state of his community. Unlike the mainstream autobiography that deals with the writer's concern with the question of identity, *The Outcaste* recounts the absence of identity itself on account of the narrator's out-caste-ness. Being aware of the fact that his suffering ensues from his status of being an *akkarmashi* or illegitimate, Limbale laments, "My autobiography holds in it the agony of such a life" and it deals with "the woes of the son of a whore" (ix). But Limbale is also aware of the fact that his condition is ultimately a result of the evil caste system that legitimizes the exploitation of Dalit women by upper caste men.

Therefore, later he comes in terms with his mother Masamai whom earlier he had looked at with contempt. He knows that his mother, like several other Dalit women, is actually a victim of the sexual desire of the upper caste men. He says "people who enjoy high-caste privileges, authority sanctioned by religion, and inherit property, have exploited the Dalits of this land. The Patils in every village have made whores of the wives of dalit farm labourers. A poor dalit girl on attaining puberty has invariably been a victim of their lust (38)." This leads the narrator to the political consciousness that the pain and agony resulting from the dehumanizing experiences of out-caste-ness, untouchability and deprivation that rip his self are the issues that affect his fellow Dalits too.

Limbale traces the trajectory of his life from birth to adulthood, carefully creating the image of his community in conflict with the mainstream social and cultural milieu. However, Dalit autobiography is not just a remembrance of things past, but a shaping and structuring of them to enable one to understand one's life and social order that wrought it. By doing so, the Dalit writer attempts to instil in the Dalit reader a passion for change. Dalit autobiography makes a shaping of the self itself since the act of narration involves the political act of self-assertion and self-creation.

E.V. Ramakrishnan, noted writer and critic, observes that there is a shift towards "graphy" and "auto" from "bio" in Dalit autobiography (98). Dalit self is constructed through the acts of violence and counter violence. *The Outcaste* is replete with instances of humiliation and oppression of the Dalits and their attempts of resistance. One such instance relates to Limbale's school days. For joining the seventh form of his neighbouring village high school, young Sharan had to apply for a scholarship. His parents and the *Sarpanch* had to countersign the application. The *Sarpanch* refused to put his signature saying that he would not approve of the name Masami Hammanta Limbale since Hammanta implied Limbale's Patil paternal lineage. He was worried about putting Patil's reputation at stake. Sharan protests, "But I too was a human being: what else did I have except a human body? But a man is recognized in this world by his caste, religion, caste or his father. I had neither a father's name or any religion nor a caste. I had no inherited identity at all. . . (59)."

Instances like this demonstrate that self-recognition in Dalit autobiography ensues from confrontation with the inimical social environment. Through confrontation with and recognition of the power structure, the Dalit self constructs itself in opposition to caste hegemony. Narration here becomes a political act of resistance because the self that narrates also interrogates the caste authority. Through the encounter with caste authority, protest against the unjust social system is inscribed in the Dalit mind, which develops into an insurgent spirit.

Unique Narrative Structure

The Outcaste is animated by a distinctive narrative aesthetics. Corresponding to the fractured and fragmented state of the protagonist's self Limbale's autobiography is characterised by an unstable time frame and dismembered narrative structure. Contrary to this, one finds a well-knit structure, linear progression and chronological time frame in Dalitist auto-narratives corresponding to the modernist perception of autobiography as a construction of history of self by shaping and arranging the things of the past. History as a continuous process of social development is a colonialist notion, which does not make any sense in the context of the subaltern, who is the real marginalized in history.

The Outcaste is organized as a recollection of multi-layered memories, layered upon one another of those moments of Sharan's humiliation on account of his half-caste existence, of want and deprivation of his people, of violation of Dalit women by upper caste men. Limbale comments: "She has to carry the rape in her womb. The rape has to be born. And this rape acquires a life and lives. My autobiography holds in it the agony of such a life (xxiv)." These memories are not arranged in any chronological sequence so as to deny them any spatial and temporal fixity and narrative logic. The narrator freely moves from one emotion to another, from one incident to another erratically, reflecting and making his introspective comments on them. The motive behind the employment of such a narrative strategy is to universalize the condition of Dalits and to showcase how the experience of the individual is a paradigm for the experience of the community at large.

Multiple addressabilities are yet other key aspects of the narrative design of *The Outcaste*. The pertinent question is who is being addressed in the text? Who are the objects of Limbale's textual utterances or for whom is the text written? Is the text addressed to the dominant castes or to fellow Dalits? Or is Limbale addressing himself as in a soliloquy, reflecting over the problems and predicaments of his self and trying to come in terms with himself? Ofcourse some of Limbale's utterances' are self-probing, "Why did my mother say yes to the rape which brought me into the world? . . . Did anyone admire me affectionately? Did anyone celebrate my naming ceremony? Which family would claim me as its descendent? Whose son am I really? (37). Such introspections foreground the crisis within the mind of the narrator on account of being a non-self originating from his half-caste status.

Limbale aptly compares himself to *Jarasandh* who is torn apart and re-joined, "I am like Jarasandh. Half of me belongs to the village, whereas the other half is excommunicated. Who am I? To who is my umbilical cord connected? (39). But some of the introspections are intended to foreground the irrationality of caste system and its inhumanity towards Dalits. The narrator wonders, "I used clean cloths, bathed every day and washed myself clean with soap, and brushed my teeth with toothpaste. There was nothing unclean about me. Then in what sense was I untouchable? A high caste who is dirty was still considered touchable! (107)."

Some of the utterances are addressed to the upper caste readers directly. Dalit autobiography demands a radical attitudinal shift from them by insisting that they should not forget their caste and class privileges. For instance, commenting on the contentious issue of caste reservation, Limbale emphatically tells the upper castes:

Those who say facilities must be cancelled should face casteism themselves. They must share the life of the untouchables. Let them live outside the village, ostracised like us. They must experience what it means to study while your father is lying drunk beside you. They wouldn't then protest against injustice. . . .Other higher - caste boys of my age addressed us derogatively, but I had to address them respectfully. My tongue itself is circumscribed by Manu's innumerable laws (90).

These words are intended to conscientize the dominant castes about the social and psychic predicament faced by Dalits. In fact the interrogative utterances with which the narrative closes are directed at the society, "Who has created such values of right and wrong and what for? If they consider my birth illegitimate what values am I to follow? (113) 'They' here may stand for the community of readers especially the upper caste, upper class readers who are the main consumers of Dalit literature. Limbale's disturbing narrative has the power to shake the reader out his/her caste complacency.

Metaphorizing the Body

Caste in the Indian context is perceived as the pre-determinant that commands norms of human behavior and bodily functions. Caste system proscribes or restricts the movement of Dalit bodies and prescribes corporal punishments for violation of its codes. Dalit body is reduced to a passive terrain where the visible codes of the caste are inscribed. It is for the same reason that Dalit writers employ body as a central metaphor, as a site of counter resistance. Limbale locates hunger as the central problem that beleaguers Dalits. In other words, frequent reference to hunger shows the centrality of Dalit body in *The Outcaste*. As opposed to the upper-caste narratives of self, where the mind or the soul of the subject and the issues affecting it occupy the centre stage, in Dalit narratives Dalit body and the experiences associated with it such as hunger and untouchability, toil and sweat get central focus. The self is intangible and fluid while the body is concrete and irreducible. The primary struggle of a Dalit is for survival. In passages dealing with hunger and search for food the narrative assumes a speed and urgency suggesting the burning sensation of hunger and the subject's attempt to satisfy it:

> We used to roam along the stream to reduce the fire of hunger in our stomachs. We caught crabs, fish, eggs, smashed honeycomb, caught birds, cried like water-fouls, tied frogs around our necks, searched for lizards, shot pebbles at kites with catapults, roasted squirrels and ate them. We went to the fields and felled leaves and fruits from trees. We broke the ant-hill and ate the queen ant (65).

A Dalit's life is an incessant struggle against the ogre of poverty and deprivation. Most of the problems in Dalit life spring from their abject poverty. In unmistakable terms Limbale shows how the terrible truth of poverty looms large in Dalit life. Sharan once

The Famished Gods

stealthily collected *jowar* (sorghum) from a corpse, which was placed along with it, as part of the last rites. Sometimes his family ate grains collected from cow dung. This is not a lone experience of Sharan and his family but the fate of the Dalits in general. Sharan recollects, "During the harvest when cattle grazed in the fields, they passed undigested grains of jowar in their dung. Santamai picked such lumps of dung and on the way home washed the dung in the river water, collecting only the clean grains. I felt the grains should not be washed as washing shrank them back (10)."

Sharan could not get even one square meal a day. Referring to hunger that haunted him throughout childhood days he writes, "My stomach was like a way to the graveyard that continuously swallows the dead (2)." Deprivation followed the Dalits at every footstep. He presents the burning problem of the empty stomach in all its gory details. It has a powerful impact on the writer's perception as it shapes his philosophical outlook on life. He says that all great ideologies come to nought in the face of burning hunger. No ideology is as powerful as burning hunger. The high-castes make Dalits subservient by controlling their bodies and its basic needs like food.

The ideology of caste system endows the high castes with monopoly on the entire resources. The lower-castes and outcastes have to render physical labour to the high-castes to satisfy their stomachs who are in turn insulted and treated as untouchables. At the end of the day Dalits are provided with only the leftover food in return for their toil. A metaphor that recurs in Dalit writings is that of the leftover food. Omprakash Valmiki, a famous Hindi writer, titled his autobiography *Joothan* which in Marathi means crumbs of food left over by high castes given to Dalits which is often thrown at them. The metaphor of leftover food frequently figures in *The Outcaste* also. Once when Sharan reaches home after eating the leftover food from his high-caste classmate, his grandmother asks him why he did not bring a portion of it and remarks that the "left-over food is nectar (77)." Dalit life writings are predominantly concerned with the representation of the concrete and the real issues that affect Dalits' daily existence. The spiritual or metaphysical issues are only secondary. This explains why 'hunger' and 'food' assumes metaphoric dimensions in *the Outcaste* as evident from the passage given below:

Bhakari is as large as man. It is as vast as the sky, and bright like the sun. Hunger is bigger than man. Hunger is more vast than the seven circles of hell. Man is only as big as bhakari, and only as big as hunger. Hunger is more powerful than man. A single stomach is like the whole earth. Hunger seems no bigger than your open palm, but it can swallow the whole world and let out a belch. There would have been no wars if there was no hunger. What about stealing and fighting? If there was no hunger what would have happened to sin and virtue, heaven and hell, this creation of God? . . . The world is born from a stomach, so also the links between mother and father, sister and brother (50-51).

Poverty is the primary reason for Dalits' subalternity and the root cause of all their problems. Limbale observes, "A woman becomes a whore and a man a thief. The stomach makes you clean shit. It even makes you eat shit (8). It is their poverty that pressurises Dalit woman to yield to upper caste's sexual advances. It is her precarious condition that forced Sharan's mother to be Patil's concubine. Sharan's life is made miserable on account of his half-caste existence; being the son of an upper caste Patil's concubine. The text delineates the gruesome details of the physical and psychic conflicts Sharan had to undergo on account of his half-caste status. As a result of his illegitimate birth he is ostracized from his own Mahar community. When he expressed his desire to marry Shewanta, his sweet heart, Santamai warns him, "The Mahars are very fierce people. They will cut you in to pieces, and there will be no one to care for us. Our house has neither a male child nor female one to continue our lives. They will force us to sleep with them. You'd better stop your affair with Shewanta (27)." Sharan being an illegitimate, both the Dalit and upper caste society treats him as an 'Outcaste'.

Reclaiming Subjectivity

According to the caste philosophy of Manu, an outcaste is devoid of soul or self and is hence inept at all scope for self-expression. Having denied Dalits of their voice and agency by relegating them to the position of mute beings, the 'Dalitist' (Dalit + elitist) writers assumed the locus of the self-appointed spokespersons of the Dalits throughout history which resulted in the distortion of Dalit voices. Dalit writing is an attempt to reclaim Dalit "selves" from the control of dominant literary representations. Put differently, Dalit narration of self is an act to assume subjectivity by reasserting their right to speak for themselves. *The Outcaste* relates the relentless struggle of its narrator against all caste odds to obtain social mobility to become a speaking subject. Through his repeated incursions into past events and his comments and ethical judgments on them, the author-narrator, breaks the centuries-old silence imposed on Dalits by the votaries of *Varna* ideology and succeeds in reclaiming his due voice and agency. This is facilitated by the choice of a self-conscious narrator who at first documents an experience for the perception of the reader followed by his reflective comments on them. This accounts for the frequent use of interrogative discourses in the text. For instance, while dealing with the discriminatory practices meted out to him by the dominant castes, narrator pauses a while to pose pungent questions, "The untouchables must not enter a temple…. We are all supposed to be children of God, then why we are considered untouchable? ….Why are we ostracized? Why are we kept away from other human beings? (62)" The profusion of sorrow and melancholy in *The Outcaste* does not undermine its predominant satiric intend, "How is a person born with his caste? How does he become untouchable as soon as he (she) is born? How can he be a criminal by birth? (82)" The narrator's interrogative comments loaded with irony and sarcasm is an attempt to lay bare the contradictions inscribed in the ideology of the dominant caste.

Denunciation of Dalit Community

While questioning the hegemonic articulations of caste, Dalit writers and thinkers often fail to critique the internal divisions of sub castes within the Dalits under the misconception that such critiquing would weaken Dalit unity. In fact the 'sanctioned silence' that they observe about the power hierarchies within the Dalits will only limit the possibility of "social revolution" and "caste annihilation" that Ambedkar had spoken about. *The Outcaste* emphasises the need for self-probing and self-criticism by speaking honestly about the inner problems of ripping Dalit community such as 'savarnization' of Dalits and practice of untouchability among the sub castes. For instance when his proposal of marriage with his friend Mallya's sister was turned down by Mallya's parents on the ground that Sharan is not of pure blood, he minces no words, "I was ashamed of this culture. I was terribly angry at its customs, but I was helpless. I had suffered the pain of insults (92)." Although he was well educated and employed, Sharan finds it difficult to get a wife from his own community. He indignantly remarks, "The girl I married needed to be a hybrid like me to ensure a proper match. A bastard must always be matched with another bastard. No one else will marry their daughters to a bastard like me (98)."

To his utter disappointment, Sharan realizes that it is not just the common folks but even the activists and intellectuals among Dalits are not free from their religious and communal biases. For instance a member of Dalit Panther group grows suspicious of Limbale on account of his relationship with a Muslim. The same fact prompts his father-in-law to quarrel with Limbale. Limbale demurs, "So a Muslim can't be my relative because of his religion is different from mine (101)." He vehemently criticizes Dalits' indoctrination into the ideology of Hinduism which is detrimental to Dalit unity which Ambedkar had stressed. Sharan wanted his marriage ceremony to be conducted according to Buddhist rituals, but Kaka insisted on traditional Hindu rituals. But being an Ambedkarite to the core when Sharan went ahead with his decision all members of his community including his close relatives like Kaka, Dada, Santamai, Masamai left the scene.

Through this incident, Limbale self-critically reveals that Ambedkar's exhortation had failed to infiltrate in to some sections of Dalit society. Ambedkar gave the clarion call to get converted to Buddhism when he found no positive action forthcoming from Hindu society to accord equal status to Dalits. In *The Outcaste*, Limbale also addresses several other issues plaguing Dalits like the assimilation of Hindu rituals, the replication of the superstitious practices of Hindu society and the subjugation of Dalit women.

Limbale also self-critically examines his own alienation from his village as he obtains social mobility, "During my college days, whenever I visited my village during vacations, I was bored. I could not tolerate the filth in my house. I had lost interest in the dreary village. It depressed me (90)." Here, Limbale focusses on the narrating self as well as the experiencing self. It is Limbale's position of being an 'insider-outsider' Dalit that enables him to fulfil the dual roles effectively.

As an outsider Limbale experiences his Dalit identity with the absence of many characteristics that he can observe in his fellow

　　　　　　　　　　　The Famished Gods

Dalits. It is his consciousness of being a privileged 'other' that renders authenticity to his narration. Limbale shares the experience of mental aloofness that many educated Dalits may feel towards their own community. His access to modern education, salaried employment, and his entry to the world of elite culture through his identity as a writer are some of the causes for his feeling alienation from his community. With his entry into the 'symbolic order' of formal language and culture, he has lost the unity and harmony that he once experienced in the 'imaginary' stage, with his community. But he is also aware of the fact that in spite of his imbibing of the 'Dalitist' (Dalit+Elitist) tradition, he has been denied access to it, a fact which enables him to get reunited with his fellow Dalits.

Limbale observes, "I was a Dalit who has become a Brahmin by attitude, but high-caste people did not even allow me to stand at their doorsteps. Either I should live in Bhimnagar, or in the Dalit locality or even in a Muslim locality. I was an outcaste in all other localities (107)." Internal probing and self-criticism are an integral part of *The Outcaste* which gives it an edge over other accomplished Dalit autobiographies like Omprakash Valmiki's *Joothan*, Laxman Gaikwad's *Uchalya*, Narendra Jadhav's *Outcaste: A Memoir*, to mention only a few. To conclude, one may say that the narrator experiences split identification at various levels – as an illegitimate, as a Mahar and even as an educated Dalit who has advanced in life compared to his community members but at the same time prohibited entry to the established social order by the caste Hindus. *The Outcaste*, thus, demonstrates the life of in-between-ness and liminality of the author-narrator.

Conclusion

The Outcaste as a Dalit autobiography puts to rest the notion that autobiography should rather belong to people of lofty reputation or people who have something of historical importance to say as Laura Marcus puts it "The Autobiography / memoirs distinction – ostensibly formal and generic – is bound up with a typological distinction between those human beings who are capable of self reflection and those who are not (31)." The wriiting of *The Outcaste* is also a moment of stock taking of the life of Limbale with all the pain, agony and excruciating experiences. It helps him to view his own life from a distance and to assess and evaluate the decisions and positions he has taken in his life. It wouldn't be wrong to say that the writing is cathartic for the author because towards the end there is a feeling of serenity, after passing through unsettling strife ridden passages. Thus Limbale, through the medium of autobiography has effected a re-inscription of Dalit cultural identity, using the locus of the Dalit insider. *The Outcaste* is a path breaking book for it marks a radical deviation from the mainstream autobiographical writings and also profoundly digresses and interrogates the depictions of Dalit life by non-Dalit writers. The sprout of Dalit autobiographies in various regional languages which followed bears testimony to the singularity of Limbale's work.

❑

                                                    The Famished Gods

About the Contributors

Deepna Rao is currently working as an Assistant Professor at Jai Hind College, Churchgate, Mumbai, and has submitted her Ph.D. thesis on the representation of 'Goan Identity in 21st Century Goan Writings' at the University of Mumbai. She holds an M.Phil. Degree from the same University with a dissertation titled 'A New Historicist Perspective of the re-writings and re-tellings of the Mahabharata in English'. She is an alumna of St. Xavier's College, Mumbai. She has previously worked as a Project Fellow with Professor Mala Pandurang, Dr. B.M.N. College, Matunga, on the U.G.C. (University Grants Commission) Major Research Project 'Wives, Mothers and Others', and as faculty at St. Xavier's College and St. Andrew's College, both in Mumbai. She has presented and published papers at both national and international forums, including a presentation on 'The Portuguese colonial dimension in the Indian Ocean re-imagined: Examining Slavery in Margaret Mascarenhas' Skin' at the University of Mauritius, co-organized by the Departments of History and Political Science, and the Centre for Research on Slavery and Indenture (CSRI), University of Mauritius, with the Mauritius Research Council, Aapravasi Ghat Trust Fund, Mahatma Gandhi Institute and UNESCO (The Slave Route Project). Her areas of interest include Indian Writing in English, Popular Culture, Nineteenth Century British and American Literature, Twentieth Century British Literature, New Historicism, Material Culture, Representation, Literary Historiography, Autobiography, Memory Studies, Ecocriticism, Gender Theory, Subaltern Studies, and Indian Ocean Arena Studies.

Surina Mol R. is an Assistant Professor in the Department of English, K.N.M. Govt. Arts and Science College, Kanjiramkulam, University of Kerala, Kerala, India. She has published various articles in many peer reviewed journals. She is interested in translation studies and has also translated poems from Malayalam. The thrust areas of her academica are Subaltern Studies, Postcolonial Literature, and Film Studies.

Sonali Rode is Associate Professor at Govt. Rajaram College, Kolhapur, Maharashtra. She has translated a poetry book from Marathi into English. She is a bilingual author. She has published four books and several research articles in International journals. Her areas of interests pertain to American Literature, Feminist Studies, and Subaltern Literature. She has received honorary D.Lit and two International awards for her literary work. Currently, she is translating Sharankumar Limbale's critical essays into Enlgish.

Darshan Lal is an Assistant Professor in Department of English, DAV College (Lahore), Ambala City, Kurukshetra University, Kurukshetra, Haryana, for the last twelve years. He has attended many National Seminars and three International Conferences where he also presented papers. He has published research papers in International Journals and contributed chapter in books. He has done his Ph.D. in Dalit Literature from Jamia Millia Islamia, New Delhi. His areas of interests are Literature in Translation (Dalit Literature), American Drama, and Indian Writings in English.

Bidisha Pal is a research scholar at the Dept. of Humanities and Social Sciences (English), Indian Institute of Technology (Indian School of Mines) Dhanbad, Jharkhand. Her areas of interest are Translation Studies, Dalit literature, Indian writing in English, Subaltern Studies, Modern and Postmodern Literature. She is presently working on her dissertation which is entitled as Role of Translation in Mainstreaming Dalit Literature: A Study of Bengali Dalit Writings. She has presented some papers in various national and international conferences on literature, language, translation, and culture. Apart from some publications in journals of national and international repute like Rupkatha, Lapis Lazuli, Gnosis, SETU etc. She has also contributed book chapters in publishing houses like Routledge, University of Illinois Press, etc.

Charu Arya is an Assistant Professor in English at Maharaja Agrasen College, University of Delhi. She has been presenting research papers on Dalit Literature, Dalit Autobiographies, Ambedkar writings and Gender writings. She has also been a Resource

Person for topics like - Studying Gender and Writings on Dalit Liberation, in Refresher Courses and Orientation Programmes, organized by UGC, Academic Staff College, Jamia Milia Islamia, New Delhi. Being a trained Linguistic Teacher, she has also taught English Proficiency courses run by ILLL, University of Delhi and has also worked in preparing materials for the same. She has been the Organizing Secretary for National Conference on Reading Migrations: Fractured Histories, Forged Narratives, organized by Maharaja Agrasen College, DU. She has also published a paper on Managing Digital Literacy in India in IJETSR. She has worked as Project Investigator in Delhi University Innovation Project titled, 'Enquiring into the relevance of Prescribed Text Books for Undergraduate Level in the University of Delhi'.

Yasmeena Jan is a research scholar at the Department of English, Baba Ghulam Shah Badshah University Rajouri, J&K, India. Presently, she is pursuing her research on Dalit Feminism. She has published her research papers in both National and International journals and has also participated in many National and International conferences.

Binu K.D. is an Assistant Professor and, Head, in the Department of English, Govt. Arts and Science College for Women Malappuram, Kerala, India. He is recognized as a Research Guide of the University of Calicut. He has been serving in various Govt. Colleges in Kerala for the last eleven years. He is the Editor of the book The Subaltern Speak: Perspectives on Malayalam Dalit Representations, published with financial assistance from Directorate of Collegiate Education, Govt. of Kerala which is the first anthology of critical essays on Malayalam Dalit Writings. His upcoming book is Articulations of Alterity: Theorising Dalit Movements. He completed a UGC minor research project titled Theorizing Pain: Constructing a Parallel Historiography of Malayalam Dalit Writings. Dr. Binu K.D. has published a number of articles in reputed National and International Journals.

Anne Placid is an Assistant Professor in the Postgraduate research Department of English, Govt. College Malappuram, Kerala, India. She is pursuing part time Ph.D. in Dalit Studies in Kerala University, Thiruvananthapuram. She has been serving in various Govt. Colleges in Kerala for the last fifteen years. She has published a number of articles in reputed National and International Journals.

Glossary

Aalekoomsalam : The Arabic greeting meaning "Peace be unto you," the standard salutation among members of the Nation of Islam.

Ahmedpur : A city in Maharashtra.

Akkarmashi : A Marathi word which means a person who is born illegitimately from parents of two different castes generally the mother from the lower caste and father from the higher and therefore an outcaste and unacceptable to the common norms of the society.

Akkalkot : A city and a municipal in Solapur district in Maharashtra.

Ambabai : A popular Hindu mother goddess.

Ambadas : The mahar boy offered to Goddess Ambabai is called Ambadas.

Anna : Addressing a brother in Marathi.

Anumana : It is one of the most important contributions of the Nyaya. Anuman a Sanskrit word, that means "inference" or "knowledge that follows." It is one of the pramanas, or sources of correct knowledge in Indian philosophy. Anumana is - using observation, previous truths and reason to reach a new conclusion and truth. A simple example is observing smoke and inferring that there must be fire.

Atishudra : In Marathi, is an individual belonging to the lower division of castes beyond the sectarian division of or the lowest rung of the society. Communities like Mahar, Mang, Chamar belong to group.

Bama : A renowned Dalit female writer of Tamilnadu.

Bauri : A dalit caste in West Bengal.

Begumpura : A name given to a fictional place which has no pain, grief, or taxes.

Bhakari : It is a round flat unleavened bread often used in the cuisine of the states of Maharashtra, Gujarat, and Goa in India along with several regions of western and central India including areas of Rajasthan, Malwa and Karnataka.

Bhau : Addressing a brother in Marathi.

Bhutalsidh : A dark deity.

Brahmin : The highest caste in the Hindu social system. They are traditionally scholars and priests.

Chappal : Open sandals.

Chaitanya : Formally known as Shri Krishna Chaitanya who was a Hindu mystic, saint, and the chief proponent of the Achintya Bheda Abheda and GaudiyaVaishnavism tradition within Hinduism.

Chaturvarna : Four Varnas Brahmin, Kshatriya, Vaishya and Shudra.

Choka Mahar : A saint poet of the Mahar community who was killed while working as an unpaid labourer in Mangalwedha.

Chuhra : Chuhra or Chura is a caste who is also known as Valmiki or Vangi caste in Northern region of India; their primary occupation was sweeping and they were considered as untouchables.

Chungi : A city in Maharashtra.

Chutney	:	It is a sauce or a dry base for a sauce, which works as a dip, relish or garnish, or an accompaniment. The word is derived from the Hindi verb translating to 'to lick' – also indicating that it is a traditionally tasty item.
Cosmic Purusha	:	It refers to the concept in the Purus Sukta of the Vastu Purush out of whose body parts the castes arose and got organized on a descending scale with lowest being dalits.
Dada	:	Addressing a brother in Marathi.
Dalit	:	The downtrodden or the lower caste. Outside the fourth category in the hierarchy of the Indian Varna or caste system and the one who is marginalized on the basis of caste.
Dalit-Panthers	:	Militant organization of young Dalits in Maharashtra formed in 1972 by Namdev Dhasal (a Dalit revolutionary poet).
Dalisthan	:	The land of Dalits.
Dandakaranya	:	The forest to which Rama, Lakshman and Sita were exiled. It is a spiritually significant region in India.
Devdasi	:	A dancer-prostitute dedicated to the deity and the patrons of a temple.
Devki	:	The biological mother of Lord Krishna who gave birth to him while in prison.
Dr. B.R. Ambedkar	:	A great luminary and parliamentarian hailed as their guiding light by the Dalit community.
Draupadi	:	Wife of the Pandava in the great epic, the Mahabharata.
Ekalavya	:	A character from the Mahabharata, he was from a tribal community and an adept archer.
Ganikas	:	Prostitutes take money for sex.

Ghatotkacha	:	The mythical giant, believed to be the son of Bhima and Hidimba.
Gondhali	:	A community of singers devoted to the Goddess Bhawani. They sing lengthy folk songs on auspicious occasions like birth and marriage, usually at night. They move in pairs: one the singer and another who plays on an instrument called the sambal.
Guru	:	A spiritual master or guide.
Guru Dronacharya	:	A character in the Mahabharata and guru of Pandavas who refused to teach Eklavya archery because of his vow to teach the offsprings from the Royal familes.
Hanoor	:	A town in a Chamarajanagar district in the state of Karnataka.
Haricha rung pahani Radhajhali dang	:	Radha was fascinated the moment she saw Hari, though he was dark.
Harijans	:	This term that was popularized by Mahatama Gandhiji for the untouchables has never been accepted by the community people. It means Men of God and for this very reason it has been contested.
Ithoba	:	A form of Lord Vishnu installed in a temple at Pandhapur.
Jai Bhim	:	A way of greeting among the Dalits who are the followers of Dr. Bhimrao Ambedkar's teachings of equality and social justice. It was first conceived and developed by L.N. Hardas (1904-1939), who was a staunch follower of Dr. B.R. Ambedkar.
Jal-Achal	:	It is a term used for the lower caste Chandala or the untouchable Dalits. It means water gets polluted and unusable if an untouchable touches it. The term has been used by Bengali

Dalit writers and novelists in their literary works. (See by Manoranjan Byapari, 2018, p. 110; the poem called or "The Untouchable Girl" by Kalyani Thakur from , 2007).

Jarasandh : A mythical character from the epic , who was invincible, even if torn asunder, his body would reunite and heal.

Jinne Amuche : It is the name of Baby Kamble's novel translated by Maya Pandit as 'The Prisons We Broke'.

Jumma ko chodu teri amma ko : Fuck your mother on Friday.

Jowar : Indian name for sorghum, with the botanical name sorghum vulgare, a food crop extensively cultivated in India. Other names for jowar include 'durra'; 'broom corn' and 'great millet'. It is a type of grass, which yields grain and fodder. The grain produces cereal that is further milled into flour used to make flatbreads.

Kabbadi : A game in which the players hold their breath while competing.

Kaka : Paternal uncle.

Karna : Half-brother of the Pandavas and Kunti's eldest son who was abandoned by her since he was born before the wedlock. Karna was raised by a charioteer called Adhiratha and his wife Radha.

Khandoba : A folk deity, reincarnation of Lord Shiva.

Khoklai : A female folk deity worshipped to cure coughs.

Kshatriya : The third highest caste in the caste hierarchy.

Kumkum : The vermillion mark on the forehead of women that symbolised their married status.

Kunbies	:	A caste or community of cultivators.
Kunti	:	The mother of three of the five Pandava brothers in the . Also the mother of Karna.
Karukku	:	This is a Tamil word which means tender or young and a text by Bama.
Lakshagruha	:	An inflammable palace made of resin designed to burn the Pandavas.
Latur	:	A city in Maharashtra.
Laxmi	:	Goddess of wealth.
Linga	:	The phallus-shaped icon, symbolising the creative power of Lord Shiva.
Lingayat	:	A community that worships Lord Verera Shiva.
Mahar	:	A so-called low caste in the hierarchy of the Hindu caste system.
Mahadev	:	A Sanskrit term meaning "greatest god," "most powerful god" or "most supreme god." It is also the name sometimes given to the Hindu god, Shiva and used as salutation in the city of Varanasi.
Maharwada	:	A locality of the Mahar community in Maharashtra.
Mang	:	A so-called low caste in the hierarchy of Hindu caste system. They are the makers of strings and ropes from hemp. They are traditionally scavengers and butchers.
Manu	:	The first man and lawgiver is attributed as the author of Manav-Dharma Shashtra.
Maryai	:	Mother goddess, supposed to ward off calamities especially epidemics
Masoba	:	A folk deity.
Masamai	:	Mother of the protagonist, Sharankumar.

Master, master		
tu kewda?	:	Teacher, teacher how big you are?
Mestizo	:	The term was used as an ethnic/racial category in the caste system that was in use during the Spanish Empire's control of their American colonies. Nowadays though, particularly in Latin America, Mestizo has become more of a cultural term, with culturally mainstream Latin Americans regarded or termed as Mestizos regardless of their actual ancestry.
Namaskar	:	A way of greeting in India by the Hindi belt people.
Neo-Buddhists	:	A term that is used to describe Ambedkar and his followers who converted themselves to Buddhism in 1956.
Nizam	:	Monarch of the Hyderabad state.
Paan	:	Betel leaf.
Pallar/Parayar	:	Dalit communities in Tamilnadu.
Panchama	:	Fifth caste in caste system referring to the lower castes.
Patil	:	A village chief/ a surname/ a member of the Maratha community in Indian villages. People having this surname are always addressed with respect as they belong to higher strata of social stratification.
Phugadi	:	A game played by young girls.
Phule	:	Mahatama Jyotiba Govinda Phule, who by his writings, created a sharp awareness about the injustices against the lower castes.
Pola	:	The ox-festival.
Potraj	:	People who are nomads and get alms for displaying an extremely grueling performance in which they whip themselves.

Rakshasi	:	A demon woman.
Ramanuja	:	He was a Hindu theologian, philosopher, and one of the most important exponents of the Shri Vaishnavism tradition within Hinduism.
Ramanand	:	Ramananda, also called Ramanand or Ramadatta, (born 1400−died 1470), North Indian Brahman (priest), held by his followers (Ramanandis) to be fifth in succession in the lineage of the philosopher-mystic Ramanuja.
Santamai	:	Grandmother of Sharankumar.
Sarpanch	:	The elected village head.
Satwai	:	A female goddess worshipped on the fifth day of the child's birth.
Shabri	:	A tribal woman in Ramayana, who offers fruits to Lord Rama after tasting them.
Shambuka	:	A shudra ascetic in Ramayana who was slain by Rama for attempting to perform penance in violation of Dharma.
Shivaji	:	Chhatrapati Shivaji Maharaj who was a great ruler in the Maratha kingdom.
Shudra	:	The fourth and lowest of the caste hierarchy.
Subaltern	:	Holding a lowest position.
Tukaram	:	He was a 17th-century Hindu poet and saint of the Bhakti movement in Maharashtra.
Tyaga	:	Tyaga or Tyagi is a caste who has a historical background of being one of the Brahmanical castes whose primary occupation was agriculture.
Vaishaya	:	The third highest caste in the caste hierarchy.
Varna System	:	System of Caste Hierarchy, where castes were divided on the basis of occupation and decided with the birth of the people.

Vithal	:	A folk deity of Pandharpur called Pandurang.
Wadaars	:	A community of stone dressers.
Waghya	:	A male devotee of Yallama, dressed like a female.
Wani	:	A business community.
Yallama	:	A female folk deity.
Yama	:	God of death.
Yuyutsu	:	A Kaurava, the son of Kshatriya King Dhritarashtra with the maid, Souvali.

References

All the chapters of this book use the following text as primary source:

- Limbale, Sharankumar. (2003). Trans. by Santosh Bhoomkar, Oxford University Press, India.

Chapter 1 : Exploring the Leitmotifs of Food

- Bhaumik, M. (2017, n.d.). An Interview with Sharankumar Limbale [Electronic Version]. Writers in Conversation Vol. 4 No. 1. pp. 3. Retrieved May 27, 2018 from https://journals.flinders.edu.au/index.php/wic/article/download/3/4
- Limbale, Sharankumar. (2016). (Alok Mukherjee, Trans.). New Delhi: Orient Blackswan.
- Mukherjee, Alok. (2016). Reading Sharankumar Limbale's : From Erasure to Assertion. In Limbale, Sharankumar & Mukherjee, Alok. (Trans.), (pp. 1-18) New Delhi: Orient Blackswan.

Chapter 2 : Inscription of Casteism through Stomach

- Agarwal, P. (2016, August 7). Caste on Your Plate: A Tale of Food Snobbery in India. Retrieved From https://www.thequint.com/news/india/caste-on-your-plate-a-tale-of-food-snobbery-in-india
- Masoodi, A. (2016, September 16). A Story of Culinary Aparthied. Retrieved From https://www.livemint.com/Leisure/wJzDhGEE4csaX2BjhjHMsL/A-story-of-culinary-apartheid.html
- Guru, G. (2009). Food as a Metaphor for Cultural Hierarchies [PDF file]. 2-27. Retrieved From https://casi.sas.upenn.edu/content/food-metaphor-cultural-hierarchies-gopal-guru
- Ichijo, A. and Ranta, R. (2016). Palgrave Macmillan.

- Kristensen, S. T. (2000). Social and Cultural Perspectives on Hunger, Appetite and Satiety. . Macmillan Publishers. 473-478
- Rege, S. et al. (2009). Pune: University of Pune (Women Study Centre). Retrieved From http://www.academia.edu/5388853/Isnt_This_Plate_Indian_Dalit_Histories_and_Memories_of_Food
- Shah, A. M. (2010). New Delhi: Routledge. Retrieved From https://books.google.co.in/s?id=EjORKo7m aRUC&pg=PA51&dq=A+M+Shah+purity+impuri ty+and+Untouchability&hl=ml&sa=X&ved=0ahU KEwiMydmaqLraAhVEM48KHVaLD9cQ6AEIJzA A#v=onepage&q=A%20M%20Shah%20purity%20 impurity%20and%20Untouchability&f=false

Chapter 3 : Hunger and Exploitation

- Gavai, R.S. (2000). Forward Note in Development of Scheduled Castes and Scheduled Tribes in India. Edited by, Jagan Karade. UK: Cambridge Scholars Publishing.
- King, Jr, Martin Luther. (1967). Where do we go from here: chaos or community? New York: Harper and Raw Publishers.
- Limbale, Sharankumar. (2003). Dilipraj Publication.
- ...(2004). Trans. Alok Mukherjee. New Delhi: Orient Longman.

Chapter 4 : A Tale of Ceaseless Atrocities

- Ambedkar, B. R. (2007). New Delhi. Critical Quest.
- Anand, Mulk Raj. (1970). New Delhi: Arnold Publishers.
- Bama. (2008). Trans. Lakshmi Holmstrom. New Delhi: OUP.
- ...(2008) Trans. Malini Seshadri. New Delhi: OUP.
- Dalrymple, William. "Serving the Goddess: the Dangerous Life of a Sacred Sex Worker." The New Yorker. 4 Aug. 2008. Web. 15 Feb. 2018.<http://https://www.newyorker.com/magazine/2008/08/04/serving-the-

goddess&hl=en-IN

- De Beauvoir, Simone. (1988). Introduction in . Trans. and ed. H. M. Parshley. London: Picador.
- Devy, G. N. (2003). Introduction in. Trans. Santosh Bhoomkar. New Delhi: OUP.
- Dhasal, Namdev. (2010) . Trans. Dilip Chitre. New Delhi: Navayana publishers Pvt. Ltd.
- Dutta, Amrita. "On a Wing and a Paper." 21 Jan 2018:6.Print.
- Fanon, Frantz. (2001) . London: Penguin Books. 1967. Rept. In Penguin Classics.
- Gaikwad, Laxman. (1998) . Trans. P. A. Kolharkar. New Delhi: Sahitya Academy.
- Gail, Omvedt, (2003). "The Downtrodden among the Downtrodden: An Interview with a Dalit Agricultural Labourer" Gender and Caste. https:// quod.lib.umich.edu/cgi/t/text/x?c=acls;cc=acls ;view=toc;idno=heb04644.0001.001 Qtd. in Girija Priyadershini. . Madurai and Chennai: Harshe Publication.
- Gupta, Monika. '. SPIEL. The SPIEL Journal of English Studies. Vol. 5. No. 1&2. Jan-July-2011. Print.
- Jadhav, R. G. (2009)., Trans from Modern Marathi Dalit Literature. Ed. Arjun Dangle. Orient Blackswan: New Delhi.
- King, Jr. Martin Luther. (1967). New York: Harper and Row Publishers.
- Limbale, Sharankumar. (2004) . Trans. Alok Mukherjee. New Delhi: Orient Longman.
- ---, . (2010) Trans. Arun Prabha Mukherjee. Kolkata: Samya.
- Mukherjee, Alok. (2010). Introduction in . Trans. Alok Mukherjee. New Delhi: Orient Longman.
- Naik, Akhila. (2007) . Trans. Raj Kumar. New Delhi: OUP.
- Panikkar, K.M. (1961) . New Delhi: Navajyothi Publishers.
- Pai, Sudha. (2013) . New Delhi: Oxford University Press.

- Thapar, Romila. (2002) . New Delhi: Penguin Books.
- Trasi, Amita. (2017) . New York: Harper Collins.

Chapter 5 : The Contested Identities

- Basisth, Divyabha. (2017). Dalit literature: An Insurrectionary Voice. .
- Bhabha, Homi K. (1994). Of Mimicry and Man: The ambivalence of colonial discourse in . Retrieved from https://prelectur.stanford.edu/lecturers/bhabha/mimicry.html
- Bhaumik, Mahua. (Interviewer) & Limbale, Sharankumar. (Interviewee). (2017). From An Interview with Sharankumar Limbale. [Interview Transcript]. Retrieved from Writers in Conversation / Vol. 4/ No. 1 /February 2017. Website: http://fhrc.flinders.edu.
- Heering, Alexander De. (2016). Dalits writing: Dalits speaking: On the encounters between Dalit autobiographies and oral histories. In Abraham JK and Misrahi-Barak J (Eds.), . (pp. 206-223), NY: Routledge.
- Kandasamy, Meena. (Jan. 2008). Articulations of Anger. Retrieved from http://www.thehindu.com.
- Limbale, Sharankumar. (2004). Trans. by Mukherjee, Arun Prabha. Hyderabad: Orient Blackswan.
- Tajfel, Henri. & Turner, John C. (1979). An integrative theory of intergroup conflict. In W. G. Austin & S. Worchel (Eds.), . (pp. 33-47), Monterey, CA: Brooks/Cole.
- Tajfel, Henri. & Turner, John C. (1986). In S. Worchel & W. G. Austin (Eds.), 'Psychology of Intergroup Relations.' (pp. 7-14), Chicago, IL: Nelson-Hall.

Chapter 6 : Voices of the Self

- Excerpts from interview with Sharankumar Limbale at National Conference held at Dyal Singh College, University of Delhi, 22 March, 2018.
- Dyal Singh College, University of Delhi, Conference on . K. Abraham, Joshil and Barak, Judith Misrahi. Eds. (2016) , Routledge.

* Basu, Tapan Ed. (2003) , Katha.
* Kumar, Raj. (2011). Orient Blackswan Pvt. Ltd.
* Zelliot, Eleanor. (2013). Navayana Publishing Pvt. Ltd.
* Rodrigues, Valerian. Ed. (2002). Oxford University Press.

Chapter 7 : Layers of Resistance

* Anandhi, S. and Kapadia, Karin. Eds. (2017). London: Routledge.
* Dangle, Arjun. (1992). Translated from Marathi Dalit literature. Hyderabad: Orient Longman.
* Gandhi, M. K. (1966). Vol. XIX. Delhi: Ministry of Information.
* Guru, Gopal. Ed. (2009) . New Delhi: Oxford University Press.
* Joshi, Barbara. Ed. (1986). New Delhi: Select Book Service Syndicate.
* Kumar, Raj. (2019). Orient Blackswan.
* Limbale, Sharankumar. Interview by Jaydeep Sarangi "Jaydeep Sarangi in conversation with Sharankumar Limbale." . 27.2 (July 2014) 39-42.
* Ramakrishnan, E. V. (1995) . Shimla.

Chapter 8 : Re-inscribing the Cultural Ambit

* Ambedkar, B.R. (1979) Vol. 1:
* Bombay: Education Dept, Govt. of Maharashtra.
* Anderson, Linda. (1998). London: Routledge.
* Gaikwad, Laxman. (1998). Trans. P A Kolharkar. New Delhi: Sahitya Akademi.
* Gandhi, Mohandas Karamchand (2018) New Delhi: Prabhat Prakashan.
* Jadhav, Narendra. (2003) . New Delhi: Penguin.
* Limbale, Sharankumar. (2004) . New Delhi: Orient Longman.
* Marcus, Laura. (1994). Manchester: Manchester U P.
* Narasaiah, Lakshmi G. (1999). Hyderabad: Dalit Sana.
* Nehru, Jawaharlal. (2004). New Delhi: Penguin Books India.

- Pascal, Roy. (1960). Cambridge: Harvard University Press.
- Rajshekar, V. T. (2004). Bangalore:Book for Change.
- Ramakrishnan, E. V. "Self and Society: Dalit Subject and Discourse of Autobiography." 33. 2. (2008): 96-109. Print.
- Valmiki, Omprakash. (2003). Trans. Arun Prabha Mukherjee. Kolkata: Samya.

Index